Once Upon a Time Out West

Once Upon a Time Out West

*For my cousin Margie
all the best!
Love, Bo*

Bo Drury

Copyright © 2009 by Bo Drury.

ISBN: Softcover   978-1-4500-0699-6

All rights reserved. No part of this book may be reproduced or transmitted in any form or by any means, electronic or mechanical, including photocopying, recording, or by any information storage and retrieval system, without permission in writing from the copyright owner.

This is a work of fiction. Names, characters, places and incidents either are the product of the author's imagination or are used fictitiously, and any resemblance to any actual persons, living or dead, events, or locales is entirely coincidental.

This book was printed in the United States of America.

To order additional copies of this book, contact:
Xlibris Corporation
1-888-795-4274
www.Xlibris.com
Orders@Xlibris.com
65232

Contents

"The Cattle Drive" 9

"A Tall Tale" 17

Albert and Betsy Lost on the Trail 23

Albert's Papa Tells a Tale 37

"The Pocketknife" 42

"Tumbleweeds" 55

"One Summer on Route 66" 61

Pier 19 64

"The Run" 70

"Ole Bob" 80

A 'Whopper' of a Tale with Adelle 82

"Writers Block" 95

"My Dad, My Hero" 98

"The Odd Box" 101

"The Move" 104

"Adrift" 109

Introduction

This is a group of short stories containing various subjects, but mostly about a boy named Albert, his adventures and the other young-uns and folks along the way. I hope you enjoy these tall tales inspired by the same told to me as I was growing up in the Texas Panhandle.

I dedicate this book to the memory of my parents, Albert and Adelle Dennis-Lockhart, who filled my life with the joys of childhood, believed in me, and encouraged me to reach for my dreams.

To my husband, Cleave, who had the patience of Job as I delved into my many ventures.

To my sons Charles, Steve, Kevin, and Danny who brought me untold happiness through the years, I would not trade a moment for all the gold.

To my nine granddaughters and five grandsons who kept me young and on my toes, and the greats who followed and extended my life.

And last, but by no means least, my grandparents who had so much influence during my young years.

Grandmother Elizabeth Mariah Kennison-Lockhart, who was so present and loving,

Grandfather CH Lockhart, who I never knew, but had so much impact on my life and I thank from the depths of my heart,

Grandmother Mabel Paulene Chowning-Dennis who taught me how to cook and sew and was my friend as well, and

Roy E. Dennis-Grandfather who I think instilled the printers ink in my veins, a man who loved words and used them.

My brother Barton, who shares my memories of days past and his wife Bobby Jean who has been my friend and sister.

My cousins Tom and Charles who were there, and my Lockhart and Dennis aunts and uncles who cheered me on,

And lastly, my best friend and 'aunt', Cherie, who taught me all I needed to know about boys.

Without them and the love shared, this book would never have come to be, for truly that is what it is all about, love of family. Written with love and a glad heart I give you . . .

"The Cattle Drive"

Albert fidgeted with his hat as he stood before his father wondering if he was in trouble. He was sure if he was, it was Howard who put him there, dad-gum him anyhow. His little brother was always getting him into a fix. He tried to remember an incident recently that would have made his Pa call him on the carpet. He looked up to see his father studying him with a grave expression. I'm in for it, he decided. Pa's blue eyes held him and the sinking feeling in his stomach was powerful.

"Al."

"Yes sir." He stood straight, shoulders back and looked him straight in the eye.

His father smiled, "Relax boy."

Albert could feel the sweat pop out on his brow and his nose itched. He wanted to scratch but he didn't dare, not now. He blinked and licked his lips. Pa leaned against the polished desk and reached for his pipe. He took his time firing it up and puffing to get it going good. All the while Al was dying a little bit inside thinking of the punishment coming. He never wanted to disappoint this man standing before him. To Albert he was a giant among men. He wanted to be just like him someday.

"I have a job for you to do Albert." He let the words sink in. "It's a man's job." His father studied the look of relief on Albert's face and hid his smile by raising the pipe to his mouth. "You're twelve years old, a young man now, you have been on the herd drives many times so you know how it's done. We have fifty head ready for market. I want you to take them in to the holding pens." Standing he walked behind his desk and pulled a packet from the desk drawer handing it to the stunned boy.

"It's a big responsibility but I know you can handle it. You will leave at first light; you should get there around dark, the stock's ready to go. You can take Ole Cap with you. He knows the ropes and will do a good job."

"Ole Cap? That old flea-bitten mutt? Just the two of us?" He protested jamming his hat on his head then yanked it off remembering where he was.

"You think you're not the man for the job?" his father questioned.

Albert caught that word 'man'. He blinked and swallowed hard, did his Pa think of him as a man now? Yesterday he was a kid getting in every-ones hair and today he's a MAN. Pa just said so. Standing tall and hooking his thumb in his pocket he answered with confidence, "Yes Sir, I am the right Man for the job."

"Fine, that's settled. Stay at the hotel and have yourself a good meal. Be sure and bring some hard candy for Howard and your Mother. She will give you a list to pick up at the mercantile. There's money in that packet to pay for your purchases." On a more serious note he added, "Do a head count along with Mr. Paxton, he will give you a receipt, bring it to me."

"Yes Sir Pa. You can count on me."

Turning he swaggered out of the room and into the yard. Once there thinking about the chore ahead his shoulders drooped. He kicked at the dirt with his scuffed up boot. Could he do it? He wasn't so keen on being a man yet, when would he have time to do the things he liked to do?

Making his way down the hill to the creek he studied on going for a swim but it was near suppertime, picking up a handful of pebbles he skimmed them over the water watching them bounce half way across the creek. "Can't nobody beat me skimming rocks, less'en its Ben."

Feeling a presence beside him he turned to see Ole Cap plop down in the shade of the cottonwood. He looked downhearted. "I suppose Pa told you about the drive tomorrow. Just you and me." he sat down beside the dog and leaned back thinking Cap wasn't too excited about going either.

He heard the dinner bell ring but his stomach felt really bad. Maybe he would get sick and couldn't go . . . He didn't think Pa would fall for that, maybe he could break a leg or arm? Naw . . . that would be too painful, maybe the Indians could kidnap him and . . . "The bell sounded again, "better get up there or Ma will have me by the ear."

His feet were heavy as he made his way to the house and washed up for supper. His appetite was gone. His Mother watched him from across the table. When she asked if he was feeling ill Pa cleared his throat and shook his head. It was no use, he had to go.

He spent half the night figuring out how he could postpone the drive but when he heard the rooster crow before the sky in the east lightened he was up and dressed.

Joining the hands at the cook-shack he grabbed a biscuit smothered in jelly and put a couple more in his pocket for later. Cook handed him a bag with beef jerky and two more biscuits as he went out the door.

The men had welcomed him as one of them and slapped him on the back as he headed for the corral to saddle up Blue-Boy. They knew it was his first trip out alone.

His big brother Ben met him at the corral and placed a rifle in the fringed scabbard on the saddle and checked out his gear as Albert put on his chaps. Albert eyed the rife and looked at Ben, "A Gun?"

"You never know when you might need one little brother. Better to be prepared on the trail. You got water in the canteen?" He worried, "And your money?"

"I'm not a baby Ben." But he was glad Ben was there. Next to his Pa, Ben was the best.

Pulling his hat down tight on his head he mounted his horse. Ben pulled open the gate and drove the cattle out of the pen. Ole Cap immediately started working the herd, running back and forth keeping the mossy-horned cows bunched. Albert looked up to see his Pa standing by the fence watching him. He nodded as Albert passed.

Scared as he was Albert made no show of it as he rode by waving his rope and herding his charges down the trail to the railway.

A ways down the trail he suddenly felt exhilarated and let out a yell that made the slow moving cows start and roll their eyes. "Ghee—Haw!"

Blue-boy bolted forward, Albert reined back on him and rubbing his neck spoke softly to settle him down, no more of that kid stuff.

The sun came up hot. Before long Albert shed his coat slinging it across the saddle horn. It was slow going; he just hoped they would get there before dark. He moseyed slowly back and forth pushing the herd forward. He had to admit Cap did most of the work.

Remembering the bag with the biscuits and jerky he decided to get down and stretch his legs while he ate a bite. Swinging off the saddle he opened the sack and shared some with ole Cap. As he sat there in the shade he eyed the rifle. Ben had taught him how to shoot and take care of a rifle but he had never had one of his own. Putting the last bite of meat in his mouth he got up and walked to it.

Taking it out of the holster he hefted it, checking its weight, then held it to his shoulder and aimed around the perimeter of the clearing. It fit just perfect, just the right size for him. The cattle were grazing peacefully on the tall grass. Cap was laying in the shade of the mesquites watching him.

As he lowered the rifle his finger closed on the trigger firing into the herd. Albert stood stock still watching as one of the big heifers sank to the ground and the others took off in a dead run Cap racing after them. Albert couldn't believe what he had done. Grabbing the reins to Blue-Boy he shoved the gun into the scabbard and jumped astride him rushing to help Cap bring the herd under control.

They were scattered everywhere. How was he ever going to get them bunched up or even find all of them in the brush? He would never get them to the rail head in time. And what about the one he killed? How could he ever face his Pa?

They searched the mesquites, but try as they would he could only find thirty-nine of them, forty counting the one he shot. He was shy ten. Wondering what he should do, take what he found on into town or keep looking, he looked to Ole Cap, "What do you think we oughta do Cap?" Cap cocked his head to one side, tongue hanging out, and barked. Albert watched the dog turn toward the herd, "Okay, lets head 'em out." Giving Blue-boy a kick they started down the trail.

They had lost a couple of hours he was sure. The sun was leaning to the west. Checking it out he noted dark clouds had built up in the north and the wind had picked up stirring the powdery dust from the trail into stinging gusts that peppered his face and arms. Donning his jacket and tying his neckerchief across his face helped but the dirt still got in his eyes.

The storm was moving in fast. He started looking for a place to hold the cattle and provide some shelter from the wind. There was no way he could hold them if lightening struck nearby. Knowing there was a creek bed off to his right he turned the herd in that direction down the embankment and out of the biting wind. The creek curved at this spot and the cattle bunched together. Albert dismounted and got as close to the steep embankment as he could. At least they were out of the wind.

Big drops of rain began to fall. Al pulled his broad brimmed hat down tight on his head and hunkered down to wait out the storm, Blue-Boy on one side and Cap on the other. The rain came in sheets. He could hear the herd but he couldn't see them but when the lightening flashed and crashed around him. He also saw the other side of the creek was running water. "That's not good." He said aloud. He put his arm around Ole Cap. He had never seen water in this creek.

Cap suddenly stood up uneasy and whined. A bolt of lightening lit up the sky and what it revealed to Albert was scary, the creek was running swift and rising fast. They had to get out. They were on the high side and to get out they would have to go into the water and find a place to climb out.

The herd had started milling around fighting to stay out of the swift moving current that swept around the curve of the creek. What Albert thought was a perfect pen for them was fast becoming a trap. He had to get them out. One look at the swirling water and he knew it was too late. He would be lucky to get out himself with Blue-Boy and Cap. He would have to depend on his horse to swim and find a place to climb over the ridge.

Heart pounding he got in the saddle. Turning to Cap he yelled, "Come on boy, ya gotta swim for your life." And he plunged into the foaming water Cap following. The reins were of no use now he thought as he wrapped his arms around the horse's neck and held on tight. He could feel the strength of Blue-Boy as he fought the pull of the water. He hoped the cattle would make it to safety.

He lost sight of Cap right off; all he could do was hang on to Blue-boy. The swift current tugged at him. With great effort he clamped his knees to the saddle worrying that the weight of the saddle and himself would drown the valiant horse as he fought to stay afloat. It seemed they traveled a great distance when Blue-boy found a footing and began the tedious climb up a slippery slope to level ground. Albert slipped off his back to lie on the ground, the cold rain slapping against him. Exhausted from the ordeal he rolled onto his stomach drawing his arm over his face warding of the pelting rain and fell asleep thinking of his Pa.

He woke to a cold nose pressed against his neck and Cap urging him to wake up. Opening his eyes he was surprised to see the bright sunlight. It was morning! He sat up looking around, Blue-boy was grazing on a tuft of grass and a dozen or more of the cattle were right past him. Cap looked at him expectantly. Getting to his feet he wondered where they were. Nothing looked familiar. He knew he had never been there before. Brushing away some of the mud from his clothes he reached out and gave Cap a hug. "Boy am I ever glad to see you."

Picking up Blue-Boys reins he stroked his neck and wrapped his arm around him. "You saved my life Blue." he leaned against him. The horse cocked his head around looking at him. Albert was sure he understood what he said. "Think you can find our way home Blue?" Putting his foot in the stirrup he swung his leg over and sat high in the saddle looking in all directions. He could find his way home or he could try to find his way to the railhead. He studied on it. He had told his Pa he could count on him.

"Round 'em up Cap lets get these 'doggies' to market." He knew market was somewhere East so they headed in that direction following the creek bed picking up strays as they went. Soon he had all thirty-nine gathered up. It was a miracle he didn't lose any more, it was going to be hard enough telling his Pa about the ten that were missing, and the one he shot!

When they reached that dreadful bend in the creek he knew where he was. The water had subsided and now only a trickle remained where once a flowing torrent of water had been. He drove the cattle across and once more they were on the familiar trail.

Albert could see the boxcars on the railway, smoke billowing from the waiting engine. He pushed the herd forward whooping and swinging his lariat. Cap joined in barking and nipping at their heels. The workers at the station saw them coming and watched the boy bring them into the pens.

"Drive them on into the cars Albert." the loader called out. "The trains ready to pull out. You just made it." A stocky man met him on the platform with pen and paper in his hand. "What was your count son?"

"Thirty-nine sir."

"What happened to the rest of 'em?"

Thinking quickly he answered, "Lost in a storm."

"Well here's the receipt. You're Pa is waiting at the hotel. He came in this morning looking for you. Better hustle over there and let him know you made it."

Surprised that his Pa was there he dreaded the meeting. It didn't give him much time to think up a good story. How could he explain about the gun and the dead cow? But wait, he really could have lost them in the creek because of the storm. No-one would ever know the difference. It wasn't his fault the storm came up and flooded the creek. He was safe as long as nobody discovered the dead carcass.

He knew he was a sight, no hat and muddy wrinkled clothes. His Pa was standing on the porch of the hotel with Ben and several men when he rode up. The look of relief on his Pa's face almost made him cry. He fairly jumped down the steps and dragged him off the horse. "Albert, what happened to you son?" He hugged him tight. It felt good but then he was a little embarrassed, after all he was getting to big to be hugged by his dad. "We were about to go look for you. Tell me what happened."

Taking him into the dinning room of the hotel and ordering him a big breakfast they all listened intently as Albert told them how the storm came up and his attempt at seeking shelter, then washing down the creek and how Blue-boy saved his life and what a good dog Cap was . . . Albert was a good story teller, always had been.

His Pa reached out and laid his big warm hand on Albert's arm. "The main thing is you and Ole Cap are okay and most of the cattle made it, we picked up ten of them coming in this morning and with your thirty-nine . . . we only lost one. I would say all in all you did a fine job and I am proud of you."

Albert sat there listening to his Pa's praise. He suddenly felt sick to his stomach. He looked at his Pa's hand on his arm and looked up into his blue eyes. Pushing his plate back he cleared his throat.

"Pa . . . about that missin' cow . . ."

© Bodrury 2008

"A Tall Tale"

Lizzie had just given the 'little boys' jelly biscuits and sent them out to play when the commotion started down by the barn. The dogs were in a panic.

"Now what?" she muttered looking out the kitchen window. "Those boys are full of mischief today. She had too much to do to put up with their shenanigans.

"That Albert, he is always instigating something."

The boys were no where in sight. Stepping to the door prepared to call out she caught her breath when she spied two dark-skinned figures slither around the edge of the barn and duck behind the hay stack. "Indians!"

Grabbing Ben's rife from its place over the door she stepped out and called in a low voice, "Albert-Howard, where are you?"

"Here Mama, under the porch."

"Stay there, I saw Indians down by the barn."

"I saw 'um to Mama, so we hid here."

Raising the rifle, Lizzie aimed toward the barn and pulled the trigger, hoping to scare the varmints off. It did nothing but stir them up. They began whooping and hollering.

"How many are out there? More than two for sure, they must know the men-folk are gone."

"Albert, take Howard and go to the cellar."

"I can shoot Mama. Give me a gun."

Lizzie hesitated, Albert was only ten, but he was stout and she knew Ben had taught him to use the gun, but he was still a little boy, her little boy. She turned as he stepped onto the porch dragging little Howard behind him.

"Get the other rifle and go to the root cellar, Hurry!"

Grabbing up Howard and rushing through the kitchen she glanced toward the big cook stove and the stew pot bubbling there, "My beans." She worried knowing they would soon need water. "They will burn to a crisp," she fretted.

Seeing Albert, she noted he had picked up the old buffalo rifle. A heap of good that will do us, she thought but it was too late to go back for the repeater. Going out the front door they circled back to the safety of the cellar unseen by the intruders.

Pulling the wooden door securely over the opening shut out the light in the earthen sanctuary. Feeling in her apron pocket for matches she ran her hand along the wooden shelf until she touched the base of the kerosene lantern. The first match sputtered and flickered out.

"Drat" She struck another against the wood. It flashed and burned bright. With trembling hands she placed the flame to the wick; it produced a soft glow as it caught fire and burned steady. Replacing the glass globe she quickly examined the contents of the small enclosure. Pulling wooden crates of apples and garden vegetables from the wall she made a place for the boys to crawl to for safety should the red devils find them there. Placing her fingers to her lips she motioned for them to remain quiet. Turning the wick as low as possible without turning it out they waited.

The crash of furniture and glass breaking sounded as the natives ransacked the house. Anger outweighed the fear she felt as she imagined her precious things being destroyed. What would be left when they were finished? The urge to face them and demand they stop was powerful but foolish she knew. Their safety was more important than the dishes she brought from Ohio. She clenched her fists and held back the hot tears.

Albert clamored past her and made his way up the dirt path to the cellar door.

"Albert. Get back here. What are you doing?"

Turning to her his brown eyes big and his mouth set in determination, "I'm going after Pa."

"No! You can't go out there, they'll see you. Come back here this instant."

He hesitated a minute as he looked her in the eye, then pushed the door ajar and rolled out closing it behind him. Lizzie lunged for the opening looking out to see him disappear into the orchard behind the house. She prayed the Indians were so involved with their destruction of her home they would not see him. Tears streamed down her face as she pulled the door shut. Taking the frightened Howard into her arms she turned the wick out. Darkness filled the room as she cradled her youngest son in her arms and hopelessly rocked back and forth weeping silently. All was lost.

Albert wormed his way across the yard than got to his knees and crawled into the trees. His heart was pounding as he made his way toward the creek behind the barn. Hearing a snort and the stamp of a horses hoof he froze and ducked down. Peeking around the brush he spied a dozen or more of Indian ponies, their leather reins hanging loose. No-one was around that he could see. If he could get to one of the horses he could ride like the wind after his Pa. He had to get help in a hurry. He pictured his Mothers face, frightened but strong, Howard had been right behind her his eyes big as saucers, to scared to speak. He had to save them; it was up to him to get help. Pa told him he was the man of the house while he was away. He couldn't let him down.

He took a deep breath and walked calmly and quickly to the first mount. The horse shied away from him, raring up his head. The other horses moved uneasily, the unfamiliar smell of him sending up an alarm. Albert moved back into the trees, unsure of what to do. Again he approached the horses, talking all the while in a soft voice. He discovered there were no stirrups or saddles only a blanket and a braided rope. Leading one of the ponies to a nearby tree he climbed up and jumped astride the frisky mount. Leaning over reaching for the reins, he raised his head and looked into the face of a returning brave, his arms loaded with some of his mother's clothes. The Brave was as surprised as Albert was.

The brave dropped the clothes as Albert kicked the paint pony and shot forward knocking the Indian aside. The other horses in a panic ran after him.

Hearing the melee, as the fallen warrior sent out the alarm, the Indians inside the house ran out to see their horses tearing through the pasture, a small boy in the lead hanging on to the horse's mane for dear life. The Indians were soon in pursuit.

Albert dug in his heels clamping his legs tightly to the pony's sides and lay over his neck, a handful of brown mane in each hand. The pony was fast and surefooted; he was far ahead of the others. Glancing over his shoulder he found a big sorrel and his dark rider closing the gap fast. Gradually changing his direction Albert headed for the river.

Once into the cover of the massive cottonwoods and thick grapevines Albert evaded his pursuers. Coming to the waters edge he pulled back on the mane coming to a halt and slipped off into the brush. Sliding into the water he hid hugging the bank. He could hear the Indians beating the brush as they searched for him. When they came near he sank beneath the surface till he felt his lungs would burst.

Remembering a trick Ben had taught him, he searched for cattails along the embankment and broke off a reed. Blowing it out, he took a deep breath and submerged. Choking he shot from the water his mouth full of the muddy river. It took a little practice breathing through the reed and staying under the water. Kicking his feet and steering with his arms he was able to move with the current downstream unseen by the searchers and continue on his way.

Coming up for air when he felt it was safe he pulled himself out onto the rivers bank. Wiping the water from his eyes he lay there. His body felt heavy and waterlogged. Emptying the water from his boots he looked around to get his bearings. How far had he traveled downriver? Climbing the embankment he looked across the empty prairie. Nothing looked familiar. He knew he was lost. Striking out for the highest point in the landscape he hoped he could see a familiar marker to tell him where he was. As he approached the knoll he aimed for, he could hear the lowing of cattle, topping the small rise he looked down on a valley filled with cattle herding slowly back the way he came from. Scanning the outriders he spotted a familiar horse and rider, a big buckskin with a tall man in the saddle, Pa. Looking further he spotted his big brother, Ben, on the red roan. He waved his arms and yelled, but no one saw or heard him. He began to run toward them.

The trail dogs spotted him first and came on the run. That caught the attention of the outriders who followed the dogs.

Albert saw his Pa stop and shade his eyes, recognizing him he came in a long gallop across the valley. The dogs reached him first, excited, and jumping all over him, knocked him to the ground. He felt strong arms lift him and looked into the face of his brother Ben.

Griping him by the shoulders, "Al, what are you doing out here. What happened to you?" he asked looking at his torn wet clothes and bloody knees.

Albert jumped up hiding tears of relief, "We gotta hurry Ben. The Indians have Ma trapped in the cellar with Howard."

He felt the security of his father's arms as he grabbed him in a bear hug, holding him close, then pushing him away. Piercing blue eyes studied his face and clothes, "What is this about Indians?"

"They tore up our house. Ma shot at them and we hid in the cellar." As he spoke the men were climbing on their horses and heading for the ranch. "Bring the boy," Pa ordered as he climbed aboard the huge buckskin and spurred him into a loping run. Ben was three lengths ahead, but Pa soon caught up and passed him.

One of the men who stayed with the cattle put albert on a horse, "Can you ride son?" asking as he handed him the reins. Albert nodded and followed the dust left by the ranch hands trailing behind his father.

The Indians were gone by the time Pa and the men got to the house. Ma and Howard were no place to be seen. "The cellar." Ben yelled. He and Pa raced for it. A hole the size of a saucer was in the door.

"Lizzie . . ." Pa called out as he lifted the wooden cover and hurried into the gloom of the shelter.

"Carl," she sobbed, "Thank God."

He gathered her in his arms. Ben picked up Howard and carried him out into the light. "Hey cowboy, you okay?"

"Albert . . ." she cried,

"He's fine, he's with us."

She looked up to see Albert standing there.

"You are in trouble young man!" she smiled through tears and held out her arms. All he could do was grin even if he was in trouble. He was really too big to be hugged by his Mama but he let her hug him anyhow.

"What happened to the cellar door?" Ben asked.

"Albert brought the buffalo gun from the house. When they came to the door I shot the gun. I thought the world had exploded down here, the boom was so loud. I guess they thought so too. They didn't come back."

"Where did you go Albert?" Howard asked tugging at his sleeve and looking up at his brother.

Placing his arm around his shoulders, Albert explained, "Well . . . I crawled to the trees . . . I found a pony and had to ride bareback . . . The Indians chased me to the river, the arrows were flying through the air . . . I crawled into a hollow log and hid . . . they were beatin' the bushes . . . then slipping into the water I breathed through a hollow reed like Ben showed us and drifted down the river. The Indians were yelling and shooting arrows at me all the time . . ."

"Were ya scared?"

"Nah . . ." They walked away, Howard hanging onto every word, as Al spun his tall tale. Lizzie and Carl laughed watching them.

"That Albert and his stories are going to get him in trouble some day."

Carl smiled. "Yep, that's my 'jelly' boy, our little hero. How much of that tale is true I wonder?" He said softly and turned his attention to the remains of the house. "Looks like we got a mess to clean up."

Entering the house, Carl heard Lizzie gasp, "Drat, those savages ate my beans."

Albert and Betsy Lost on the Trail

The first rays of sunshine had lightened the sky and then burst forth, its red gold rays casting far reaching shadows across the sleepy camp. Libby and several other early risers had come to the fire to warm.

"It's going to be a beautiful day." Carl remarked looking at the red glow of light in the east.

Looking up and taking in the brilliant sight Libby shook her head." Remember what the sailors say . . . . red sun in the morning . . . sailors take warning . . . ."

She smiled at him then turned serious as she looked back towards the area where the stock had been bedded down.

"What's wrong with that cow? She's been putting up a fuss all morning, woke me up before daylight.

Looking toward the second wagon she called out." Albert . . . hustle up and see what's wrong with ole Bossy, son."

"It's the smell of those wolves prowling around, I'm sure it makes her nervous about the calf." Carl allowed.

"You think they would come in this close?"

"The dog would set up a howl if they did." he assured her." I've noticed old Cap is hanging in close though. He wants no part of that pack of wolves."

Albert climbed down from the wagon, none to happy about being rousted out of his warm bed to check on the dumb cow.

"May as well milk her while you're at it, Albert." His mother said handing him the milk pail," It'll go good with these grits." she said stirring the bubbling broth over the fire.

There was no doubt, in any ones mind, that Albert was disgusted as he stomped away in the direction of the cow, muttering under his breath as he went.

Pouring Carl another cup of coffee Libby remarked," She's quieted down already. Maybe she was just lonely."

They all looked up as Albert came hurrying back.

"Bossy broke the rope and ran off into the woods. The calf is gone."

"Darn those wolves." Carl stood up," get your snow shoes on and see if you can catch her. No time to look for the calf. Probably couldn't find it anyway. We'll get moving as soon as you get back."

Albert grabbed a biscuit and stuffed it into his mouth, then picked up two more and put in his pocket as he hurried away.

"I'll save you some breakfast." his mother called after him as he hurriedly donned his snow shoes, and sheep lined coat. He wrapped a scarf around his head and face and trudged through the thick snow in search of Bossy. Ole Cap leaping along behind him. The cold made his eyes tear up and his nose turn red.

"That darned dog will not be any help getting Bossy back, probably run her further into the woods." Carl said watching after them.

No one noticed a few minutes later when Albert's little sister, Betsy, bundled up in her coat followed in the tracks of her big brother.

Albert didn't go far before he figured out there were feet print other than his or Bossy's in the snow. He studied, should he turn and go back, or try to catch Bossy before someone else did? Those prints were made sometime in the night.

Wolves didn't get that calf, it was Injuns!

Those sneaking redskins! He decided he better get a move on and catch up to Bossy. He was sure Ole Cap would warn him if he got close to the Indians. He was bounding ahead looking for game. He would stop now and then to sniff the tracks ahead and then off again he would go. Albert soon lost his fear of what lay ahead thinking they were surely long gone. He had only catching Bossy to worry about.

Twenty or thirty minutes into the woods he thought he heard someone call his name. He stopped and listened. Must be the wind . . . wait he heard it again. Faint and far off. He turned and listened intently.

"Al . . . bert." called out a small voice from somewhere behind him. He retraced his tracks and there he found Betsy . . . worn out from trying to catch him. Tears streamed down her face.

"I couldn't find you." she said accusingly. "You take to big a steps." she cried

"Betsy, what in the world did you follow me for?" He picked her up and wiped her nose and tears.

"You found me, don't cry. Did you tell Mama you were going?"

He wondered then if he should take her back or keep after the cow. It was going to delay their travels for this day . . . but he knew when they missed Betsy, they would be in an uproar. He thought about it for a few minutes then decided to hurry on taking her with him. He hoisted her to his shoulders and started off. Ole Cap had come back delighted to see little Betsy along.

Suddenly he stopped. The hair on his back stood up like a wire brush. He emitted a low deep growl and stood stock still.

Albert heeded the warning and squatted down holding Betsy close. He put his fingers to his lips and warned her not to make a sound. Betsy's eyes grew large as she watched, first her brother and then Ole Cap. She was smart enough to know when to be still.

Albert reached out and put his hand on the dog, hoping he would not give them away. It was the Indians coming back. He knew they would soon reach his tracks. He could just make out their voices as they neared. They too heard the small voice call out and had come in search of it.

They would have to make a run for it. He whispered to Betsy,

"Hold on tight—don't make a sound . . . its Indians." Betsy threw her arms around Albert's neck and squeezed her eyes shut. He could feel her little heart pounding.

He stood quietly and took a few steps, then bending low he began to run. Ole Cap ran with him, soundlessly, as if he knew the peril they faced. Suddenly he heard the loud jabber of the Indians . . . they had found them out. Now the chase was really on.

He didn't know which way he was going . . . toward the wagons or away. He was leaving tracks he knew. He had to get out of the snow somehow so he could lose them . . .

They happened upon a small stream with rushing water. He would have to go in. He could hold Betsy up out of it, he didn't have time to give it much thought. He plunged into the icy water . . .

Ole Cap stopped, whined, and ran back and forth along the bank. Finally he too leaped in to go with Albert. They turned down stream. He hoped they couldn't tell which way he went.

Ole Cap scrambled out of the water onto the bank. He ran along keeping pace with the slender boy . . .

Betsy was heavy and had a death grip on him. His legs were numb from the cold water. He wondered how much further he could go like this.

He didn't hear anything behind him. He stopped to listen but all he could hear was the rushing water as it swirled around his legs. He went to the bank and sat Betsy down and climbed out. He was half frozen. He couldn't feel his feet.

It was rocky here and he felt they would be safe to leave the water. It would be harder for them to track he hoped, thinking of the Indians that pursued them.

He wondered if the folks had missed Betsy yet. Maybe someone would notice the tracks of the Indians and come looking for them. Betsy had still not made a sound. He pulled her close, to comfort her and warm himself. Ole Cap snuggled in on the other side his eyes watching for any movement in the brush.

Albert knew he had to keep moving, get some circulation going in his legs. He lifted Betsy once again and put her on his back. "Hold on." he ordered as he stepped from rock to rock, hoping to leave no trail behind.

Deciding they should follow the stream for safety, they made their way along the rocky bank. He could always take to the water again if need be, as bad as he hated the thought.

He had not noticed the big dark bank of clouds that gathered in the northwest. There was no way for him to know, too, that with each step, he moved further away from his family. His only concern now was staying ahead of what he thought was sure death for them both.

He had overheard the talk of the men folk around the fire at night as he lay in his bed. The stories that they told of the fierce and savage Indians made his hair curl and put shivers in his spine.

He knew what the Indians did to white women and girls they took. They would have no use for a boy like him, unless they made a slave out of him, they would more than likely torture and kill him, probably after they scalped him. He couldn't help reaching up to feel his thick hair.

They would steal a little girl like Betsy and make a squaw out of her. He couldn't let that happen, no matter what.

Stopping to rest a minute, he looked at his little sandy haired sister. She would be pretty, like their Mother when she grows up, he thought.

"I'm hungry, Albert." she said in a small voice. He looked at her in surprise.

"I bet you are," he replied." We didn't get to eat breakfast." He remembered the biscuits he had in his pocket. They were probably ruined by now he thought but when he pulled one out it was still intact.

"Here I'll split this with you" as he realized he too, was hungry. He decided to save the other one. He was glad his mama makes extra big biscuits.

About to take his last bite, he noticed Ole Cap watching and wagging his tail expectantly. He hesitated only a moment before giving it to him. Cap had saved them. In Albert's eyes he was a hero. He rubbed his head . . . "Good Boy." he said affectionately.

Its way up in the day he thought looking at the sky. They must be looking for us. (The folks he meant.) Maybe we should just sit still and wait for them to come. He wished he had a gun or even a knife.

Pa had given him a knife, telling him to always keep it handy, but he had left it in the wagon where he was whittling on a little flute made from a hollow reed.

He had practiced shooting the gun brother Ben gave him and was really pretty good, but all that didn't help him here with no gun. He felt so helpless. He didn't even have his sling-shot, plenty of rocks but what could he do with those?

The sun shone down on them and it was warm. Betsy laid her head against him and fell asleep, might as well let her rest a little while. Ole Cap will let me know when its time to move. He dosed of too as he grew warm and his feet thawed out.

The leaves stirred around him. First just a few, then a breeze picked up and begin to blow steady, still Albert and Betsy slept. The gray clouds began to scud across the sky and it grew dark.

The north wind had a chill in it. Albert woke suddenly as the chill in the air penetrated his clothing. He sat up surprised at the condition of the sky. It had been sunny only a little bit ago. Where was Cap? He looked all around . . . That mutt was nowhere to be seen. Betsy opened her eyes, sleepily looked about and declared she needed a drink.

You'll have to drink out of the stream of water."

"How?" She replied.

"Here let me show you," he lay down with his face in the water and drank thirstily.

"Like that." he explained.

Picking her up he held her face down over the water. She began to kick and squeal.

"Betsy, Stop. What's wrong with you?"

"You trying to drown Me." she cried.

"No . . . you have to lay your lips in the water and slurp it up." he explained. "I won't drop you in the water."

Still she struggled against him, terrified of the rushing water. He sat her down and walked a ways down the rocky stretch looking for a place where the rock was level with the stream.

"Here." He called" this is a good place. You can drink with out me holding you. She came forward, doubtful.

"Lie down on your stomach and put your lips to the water, then suck it up!" he coached . . . He watched her but also kept his eyes pealed for Ole Cap.

Now where would he get off to? I didn't think he would leave us. I hope the Indians don't catch him. He worried.

They had to find a place out of the wind. There was no way to make a fire and it would be dark before long. Taking Betsy's hand they left the rocky embankment and walked into the woods.

There was snow but also places under the trees where the snow was gone. It had either melted or the trees were so thick it couldn't hit the ground.

He found an outcropping of boulders with an overhang of brush on it. It was protected by the trees as well. They crawled into the hollow of the rock.

Albert thought about his Pa's stories about owls and crawly things. After checking it out and finding no creepy crawly things, he pulled a bunch of dry leaves into the depression to make a soft bed and taking off his big coat he prepared to snuggle down with Betsy until daylight. It wasn't quite dark yet and he noticed a star twinkling through the clouds. That must be the evening star, the wishing star. He wished they were back at the wagon safe and warm.

Pa needs to teach me how to tell direction by the stars he thought. Feeling in his pocket he found the second biscuit.

"Here Betsy" he teased" lets pretend we are having a picnic."

He broke off half and divided it with Betsy and carefully put the other half in his pocket.

The clouds closed in and the wind blew. Soon snow began to fall again. Albert and Betsy snuggled in the dry leaves beneath the sheepskin coat.

He wished for Ole Cap, Betsey wished for her Mama, but she didn't cry, she had Albert and she knew he would take care of her.

Shortly after Albert left, Libby called for everyone to get up and come to breakfast. One by one they gathered around the fire still sleepy headed.

The men had started hitching up the teams to the wagons and preparations were under way to get an early start as soon as Albert got back with bossy.

Noticing that Betsy was not there with the girls, Libby told Alice to fetch her.

Surprised she answered "She's not in the wagon, mama."

"What do you mean she's not there . . . where is she?"

"Why I don't know" The girls looked at one another. Libby went to the wagon and climbed inside moving the bedding around.

"Now where is that little minx?" Climbing out She looked over the camp.

"Carl," she called "Have you seen Betsy?"

"Not this morning" he replied" is she hiding from her mama" he smiled as he finished with the harness.

Turning to Libby he winked, "Wonder where our little Betsy is . . ." and he sneaked around the wagon.

"No Carl . . . she is not in the wagon . . . I can't find her in camp."

Straightening up Carl looked at his wife, "What do you mean . . . she's gone?"

With sudden panic, she realized that what he said was, in fact, true, Libby whirled around and cried out.

"Betsy!" She screamed.

Immediately the whole camp was at her side. Everyone began the search.

Shortly one of the men called Carl aside.

"Looks like we had company in the night . . . There are moccasin prints where Bossy was tied. They lead off into the woods."

"Here are her feet prints . . . she followed Albert." someone called.

"Don't say anything to Libby about what you found . . . not yet." Carl said hoarsely. Turning he made his way quickly to the wagon where Betsy's little prints were showing in the trail after her brother.

"Albert will look after her." He assured her, placing a comforting arm around her.

"At least we know where the little rascal is." He looked after the trail with a troubled face. "Perhaps some of us should go along to help Albert. He will have his hands full with Betsy and Bossy"

"He motioned for the men to come with him. "Might take a rifle along to see if we scare up any game."

While the men went after their rifles Carl pulled a couple of the cowboys aside and told them what had been found . . .

"Stay with the women and keep a close watch. Try not to alarm them right now. We'll see what's going on soon enough."

Going back to Libby he told her "Ole Cap is with them. They're in good hands" he joked. "We will be back shortly," with that the three of them headed into the woods following the trail Albert had left.

Traveling at a fast pace it wasn't long before they intersected with the place Albert had come back for Betsy. It was plain the Indians had been there also.

Did the Indians have them or did the kids get away. Carl was stricken with agony. His children in the hands of savages, he couldn't believe this was happening.

"Get a grip Carl. Looks to me like Albert went out this way ahead of them." Doc studied the ground." He must be carrying Betsy . . . here are Ole Caps prints. He is running along with them."

Given hope, Carl pulled himself together.

"Lets go." He said, following the obvious trail left by the Indians. They lost the trail several times and had to back track. Seemed the warriors had as hard a time reading tracks as they did.

"I haven't seen any sign they caught up to him yet." Doc said

"I'd say that boy can run like a deer." Carl's friend Harvey said, shaking his head in admiration. "He sure had those Indians going in circles trying to catch up to him, and him carrying little sister."

When they got to the creek they could see that the Indians had split and gone in either direction. There seemed to be only three of them. One had crossed the creek in search of Albert's tracks coming out on the other side. One had gone upstream and the other down. Seeing for them selves that they had not crossed over and come out on the other bank, they studied about which way the kids had traveled.

"I think Al would know that going up stream would be easier to track." Carl mused.

"We need to split up." Doc suggested.

"I think we need to stay together. No telling what we may run into." Harvey argued.

"It's taking to long." Carl worried." we have to keep to their trail. If they find them first . . . ." he didn't want to think of that.

He looked at the sky. They had been in these woods for hours searching for them. He saw the big dark bank coming from the north.

"We have to find them before that storm comes in . . . We'll lose all sign then."

Doc still studying the ground turned to them "The one that went downstream came back this way from these tracks . . . so the kids must have gone upstream."

"That surprises me." Carl replied" I guess he didn't have time to give much thought to which was the best way to go."

The three men started off upstream at a brisk pace, yet with caution, rifles ever ready. They stopped often to listen, hoping to hear a call for help, or a dog bark, anything that would give them some hope the kids were still ahead of their pursuers.

The clouds began to move in and the winds picked up. They could feel the chill in the air and knew they were in for a storm. They pushed on searching.

Harvey, who had taken the lead suddenly stopped, holding up his hand. He had heard voices ahead. Carl and Doc came forward, they could smell wood smoke. They got down on their hands and knees and approached the Indians camp. There were three figures hunched around the fire. They were talking and gesturing in different directions with their hands, seemingly upset about something.

Carl scanned the area in search of the children. There was no sign of them. Evidently they had escaped much to the frustration of the Indians.

Relieved, they silently backed away.

"What now?" Doc asked of Carl.

"Forget them. Let's get after the kids. It's getting late. We need to find them before this darn storm hits us full blast." He answered. They began to retrace their steps.

"Maybe their back in camp by now . . . Once they got away that's probably where they headed." Harvey offered hopefully.

"Could be." Carl replied looking again at the darkening sky. "We'll go back. You're right. Albert won't want to get caught out in this. He'll have headed back to the wagons as soon as he lost them."

With that they started in the direction of the camp.

Half way back they heard the bawling of old Bossy. Following her crying, they came upon a small clearing. Bossy stood by her calf. He had been tied to a tree. She was trying her best to get him to follow her. The remains of a burned out campfire were near by. Evidently Albert had disrupted them in the process of planning a fine meal. Untying the hungry little fellow Doc took hold of Bossy's lead rope and led the way toward the wagons.

Libby saw them coming leading the cow and calf. She ran forward a smile of welcome on her face.

"They're back" she called out joyfully . . . then stopped when she realized the children weren't with them.

"Carl . . ." her voice faltered.

"Their not here." he stated. It was a question.

"Oh my God . . ." she wailed hugging her arms to her body and sinking to the ground.

Carl went to her, kneeling and taking her in his arms.

"We'll find them. Albert is a smart boy, he knows what to do." he tried to consol her. He would have to tell her about the Indians.

Snow flakes had begun to fall. It would soon be dark. It would be impossible to look for them now. All they could do was to build a big fire and keep it going through the night, hoping it would guide them home, if they were out there. Carl felt sure Albert would find a shelter and stay there 'til morning.

It was a quiet group that gathered round the fire for an evening meal. Libby wouldn't even try to eat, thinking of her children out there someplace cold and hungry . . . She paced back and forth through the snow and wind. Carl made her put on her wraps and bundle up from the cold.

She was oblivious to all that went on around her. She watched the dark woods, hoping vainly they would appear. Nothing anyone said consoled her. Carl watched her, waiting for her to collapse, but she showed no sign of tiring. They continued to feed the fire, taking turns.

The wind blew and the snow drifted against the wagons. The fire provided little heat, as the wind blew against it. They put up a makeshift shelter and gathered behind it, for what warmth they could capture.

Sometime in the night Carl had dosed off when he heard Libby call out. He jumped up, expecting to see her lying prostate on the ground, but rather found her with her arms wrapped around the scruffy body of Ole Cap.

"Cap . . . oh Cap where are they?" she cried looking past him in the direction where he had been.

"Good boy," She crooned and rocked as she held him close and wouldn't let go. The dog began to squirm to be free.

"As soon as it's light he can take us to them. It won't be long now." Carl told her.

"The snow will cover his tracks before we can see them." Harvey worried.

"We'll let him lead us to 'em."

"You think he can do that" Doc asked.

"I think that's what he came to do. Otherwise he would never have left Albert." Carl replied.

"You're putting a lot of faith in that old cur dog, Carl." Doc said skeptically eyeing the dog.

"Give him a bit to eat and some water. I think he is raring to go back already"

"We can't go 'til first light anyhow." Carl said with regret. "But let's be ready."

Turning to Libby, he said gently, but forcefully." You get in the wagon and get warm. You need your strength and your wits about you. You have the other children to think of, too. When we go for Betsy and Albert, it's up to you to look after the rest of the families. The men will go with me, you will be in charge."

Giving her responsibility he hoped would help keep her mind occupied.

* * *

The snow drifted around the boulder creating a wall that shielded the wind from Albert and Betsy as they slept. The snow gathered on the overhang of brush and as it deepened it draped over the front of the depression enclosing them in their shelter. Their body heat beneath the big sheepskin coat kept them warm in their bed of leaves. He woke once in the night, remembered where they were and pulled Betsey closer. Then fell back into a deep sleep.

* * *

Before the sky had lightened the men of the camp were already tramping through the woods following the sturdy old dog. He appeared to know where he was going and what they expected of him.

From time to time he would stop, look back impatiently, to see if they followed and continue on, seeking a trail through the thick brush and trees. It was hard for the men to keep up with him.

At times they couldn't help but wonder if they were on a wild goose chase. They felt they were going in circles. With no sun to guide them and snow still falling heavily, it had to be instinct that showed the dog the way.

They could be lost themselves, but for Ole Cap. They came once again to the stream of water but none of it was familiar. Cap seemed to hesitate, looking in either direction, then turned down stream. Carl thought to himself, I knew he would choose this direction.

They walked for what seemed miles. Further into the woods, skirting boulders and brush. The dog kept on, not slowing his pace. The men were beat. Suddenly he stopped and whined looking back, then ran ahead to disappear around a huge outcropping of rock.

The men had to line out single file to follow through some narrow crevices. Cap was waiting for them when they got through, then he dodged beneath some snow covered branches, barking. The men heard a clear voice exclaim,

"Cap . . . where have you been . . . look out your getting snow all over us . . ."

They heard Betsy squeal and laugh as the wiry mutt scampered over them in excitement.

"Albert . . ." Carl called out . . . there was a brief silence before he answered

"Pa is that you . . . ?" Disbelief and joy in his voice.

"It's me boy." his voice cracked with emotion as he pulled aside the brush barrier and looked inside the small cave like niche.

"Poppa" Betsy squealed throwing her self into her daddy's arms.

"How did you find us" Albert asked putting on his big coat.

"We have to thank this mangy ole mutt for that. He's a real hero I'd say. "Reaching out to rub the dogs head" Let's get home to your Mama. She's bout sick with worry over you two." He said gruffly as he gathered Betsy up in his arms and turned to the men with him. They were all smiles. Albert was surprised when he came out to see all the men from the camp with his father.

"We looked for you yesterday. Saw where the Indians chased you but we lost you at the creek." Doc grinned" So did they . . ."

"I'm hungry Poppa." Betsy said placing her little hands on his cheeks, turning his face to look at her.

"Here Betsy" Albert held out the piece of biscuit he had saved," that will have to do 'til we get home. Then we can have some real food."

A light snow was still falling when they returned to camp. Anna saw them first.

"Mama"

Libby, bent over the fire stirring a pot of beans, looked up at her daughter. She couldn't make out the meaning of the expression on her face, Joy . . . fear . . . She whirled around ready for anything and there they were. The color left her face and her hand went to her breast. She was speechless . . . then the tears of relief and joy poured forth as she ran to gather them both in her arms.

Ole Cap was dancing around for attention as well, leaping up and barking. It was a glad and happy crowd that welcomed them home.

Albert and Betsy keep them entertained all evening with stories of their misadventure. Libby looked on eyes brimming with love and a joy-full heart. She held Betsy close and looking skyward silently gave thanks.

Reaching out she clasped Carl's hand in hers as she listened to Albert tell excitedly about their experiences in the wilds of the woods. It had been a good day she thought as she watched Ole Cap lay down at Albert's feet and his hand drop down to ruffle the thick hair on his neck as he talked. What a picture . . . A boy and his dog . . .

© bodrury2007

Albert's Papa Tells a Tale

As all children do, Albert and his brothers and sisters loved to hear the stories their father would tell as they sat around the fire on cold winter nights munching pop corn and sipping hot cider.

"Tell us Papa, please do. Tell the one about the night grandpa disappeared."

Unable to resist the chance to tell a tall tale Carl lifted little Betsy to his lap and looked around the room at His children. Sure he had their attention he began:

"Well . . . when I was but a lad of nine or ten," All eyes were upon him. "I was awakened in the dark of night. My father shook my arm . . . but shushed me . . . be very quite, he says in a whisper. Gather your sisters and follow down the stairs with me."

"What is it Father?" I asked, but he did not hear me. I quickly shook my sisters and we tiptoed down the stairs in our night cloths . . . One of the steps squeaked . . . My father swung around. "No noise." he whispered.

We were fair shaking with fright, the way he was acting. Then . . . we heard voices."

Papa stopped and put his hand to his ear, "Listen" he whispered, everyone around the fire strained forward unconscious of their movement.

"We could hear voices outside our house. They sounded rough and mean.

I was shaking in my shoes.

37

"It's the French," Father whispered, "I must hide you . . . come." And he led us into the fireplace room. There he removed the rug from in front of the hearth and raised a trap door.

Now I never knew that door was there in all those years. And I was nigh-on-to ten years old. What a surprise."

Papa leaned back on his seat and raised his brows in mock surprise letting out a little gasp.

He looked around at his audience, and leaning forward with an air of urgency went on;

"We quickly descended the steps to a room beneath our house. Why was there a room under the floor of our home I wondered? I looked around but before I had a chance to see anything . . . Someone began to beat on our door, demanding to be let in."

"Open up this door" they shouted. My father put his finger to his lips . . . shhhh . . . he said. They continued to shout. Then they beat on the door to break it down.

There were guns in the room with us and father picked up a rifle and handed it to me and he took one for himself. He then belted two pistols around his waist.

That rifle he handed me was near as heavy as myself. What was I to do with it, I wondered?"

Papa leaned back and got out his pipe. He tamped tobacco carefully into it and leaned toward the fire to get a twig to light it. It took a few minutes to get it going. He took advantage of this time to look around the fire at all the expectant faces. He loved it, the ability to capture their attention like that.

With a puff and a smile he went on.

"Now there was another door in this room. When father opened it, it appeared to be an old storage room but when he removed some of the junk we could see there was another opening going through it

"Carl . . . he said . . . I'm counting on you to see to your sisters safety. You take this gun and if anyone tries to stop you, shoot them. Do you understand what I am telling you, son?"

"Yes sir." I said, loud and clear.

He gave my sisters' shoes and a shawl and me an old jacket that was twice my size.

It made me feel like I was a man. I had on a pair of old boots that I found in that closet.

Then father said . . . "This tunnel will lead you out into the woods. Be careful when you come out. Don't make a sound. Don't be scared. You will be OK. I'm counting on you son." He said to me then turned to the girls, caressed their cheeks, and pressed his lips to their forehead, "You girls do what your brother tells you too do. He's in charge." He paused and looked at each of us, as though to record it in his memory, He looked sad, it made me scared to leave him.

"It's a long way, but run to your Uncle Ben's. Stay in the woods, lest they find you, now go . . ." he said pushing us through that dark opening. It was dark as pitch in there. We had to feel our way out. It took a long time.

There were all kinds of creepy crawly things in there with us. Spiders and rats"

Papa shivered, making a show of shaking all over.

The women and girls looked around and pulled their skirts closer to them,

"We finally came out into the night air. It was cold. The old hooty owl was hooting and screeching at us, it sounded spooky. Then we heard things crawling around in the bushes . . . we didn't know if it was the French or not. It felt like something was about to reach out and snatch us up. We took off running into the woods. I had to grab Molly by the hand and drag her with one hand while I held the rifle with the other. Sarah was right behind me. Both of the girls were crying.

"Shhhh . . . I said. Don't be a cry baby."

Papa stopped for a minute,

"Is there any more of that cider? This story telling is hard on my throat," he said.

"Oh . . . Poppa . . . hurry up, what happens next?" Anna asked impatiently.

Papa waited as Alice got him a cup of cider and settled back in her place by the fire, then went on.

"Well we wandered around all night in the dark. We didn't know where we were. I didn't know then that you could tell direction by the stars.

Finally we got so tired we had to stop and rest. We sat under a big tree with our back against it so nothing could reach out and grab us.

The girls fell asleep but since I was the man in charge I had to stay awake. My eyes felt like they wus buggin' out trying to see in the dark. Every little sound I moved my rifle in that direction ready to shoot.

Then all of a sudden there was a terrible racket . . . something' coming right at us . . . I raised my rifle and prepared to meet the enemy . . . I saw this huge big monster of a man coming at me . . . I knew he was the French . . . I took careful aim and slowly pulled the trigger. BOOM . . . that gun knocked me back against the tree and knocked me out. I felt myself sinking . . . I knew I was dead for sure . . ."

"What happened then?"

"I woke up . . . it was a dream."

"Papa . . ."

"Time for bed little ones . . ." Mama, laughing, stood up and waved the children toward their beds.

"That was awful, Pa," Albert said as he tramped off.

Papa lit his pipe again giving it a puff. Mama sat beside him,

"I wondered how you were going to get out of that tale." She questioned. "I think you had them going, sounded pretty good, might have believed it myself."

He smiled and took a puff at his pipe. "That was a scary night. I will never forget it. I could have told them that the big scary monster I shot at was a big scared raccoon and that I nearly scared us all to death when I pulled that trigger."

"Well you were the oldest, but that was a lot to put on a little boy."

"Yes and I was scared spit-less. They all thought someone had shot me when they ran over to find me lying under that tree. The blood from my nose, where the gun kicked back, was all over me. They thought I was dead."

Papa chuckled as he sat there quietly, remembering.

After a few minutes he said, "That was a long time ago, another lifetime."

After a brief silence,

"I'll always wonder what happened to my father. We never saw him again."

Lost in his thoughts, Papa suddenly broke the spell when he stood up and stretched.

"Let's turn in Mother. Good night Albert . . . I know you are listening . . . I'm glad you did."

"Me too." Albert answered as he walked out of the shadows and into the light of the fire.

Papa knocked the tobacco from his pipe and headed for the warmth of his feather bed . . . It had been a good day, a good story, a bit of history passed on. Albert climbed the stairs and fell across his trundle bed.

Looking through his window at the stars twinkling in the clear cold sky he wondered where his grandpa might be.

Out there someplace under the same stars that shone down on him this night, fighting the French, and maybe an Indian or two?

© Bodrury 2008

"The Pocketknife"

Anyone paying attention would think they were just watching a boy on an old nag riding down the road late one evening. They wouldn't know they were watching a runaway, a boy mad enough to spit nails.

Mumbling as he rode along Carlo fought the tears that persisted in gathering in his eyes. "He would show them." he said. His backside still smarted from the sting of the bull whip his Pa had used on him.

He never stuck Anna with a pin like she claimed, but Pa always believed her over him. "Well, that would be the last time." he vowed as the road before him swam on unshed tears.

He had gathered his few belongings, rolling them in his blanket, and saddling up old Tony had set out for parts unknown. He didn't have a plan, he just knew he wasn't hanging around there any longer and taking a lick for something he didn't do.

Boy, he hated that stuck up Anna. She was always getting him in trouble. Pa was partial to her over the rest of them. Everyone cow-towed to her, even Mama it seemed, but he was fourteen now and too old to be getting licks. He was going out west and making his fortune. They would regret the way they treated him then.

The late afternoon sun cast long shadows across the road then dropped behind the low hills ahead. Carlo's stomach growled and gurgled reminding him it was way past suppertime. He thought about the big biscuits his Mama made and the plum butter she had put up last summer. His mouth watered as he remembered the fried chicken and mounds of potatoes he usually had on his plate.

Boy, he was hungry. He wished he had thought to bring along a cold biscuit or two. He didn't have a penny to his name. Where was he gonna get something to eat? And where was he going to find a place to spread his blanket?

Leaving the road he began looking for a likely spot along the creek. Maybe come morning he could catch his-self a fish for breakfast. Removing Tony's saddle, he placed it next to a big cottonwood along the bank and laid his blanket over it using it as a pillow.

For the first time he thought of his horse and the fact he had nothing to feed him. He would just have to eat grass. Carl wondered how grass would taste. He was hungry enough to try it himself.

Laying down he looked up through the leaves and studied the stars. There were millions of them up there.

He wondered if anyone had missed him yet. Would his Mama cry for him? He listened as the frogs and crickets began their evening song, he had never noticed before how sad and lonely it sounded.

Carlo woke to sunshine filtering through the leaves and playing patterns on his face. Tony grazed nearby. The water was calm; there was hardly a ripple in it. Swamp flies were skimming along its surface. A fish leapt from its depths and snatched his breakfast in flight.

Thinking of how hungry he was, he grabbed up his boots and quickly pulled them on, then looked about for a stick to fashion a spear.

He always carried the pocket knife. He got it for Christmas when he was eleven. It was a treasured gift from his Pa. He studied on that for a minute and then shaking his head said aloud, "He never should have hit me with that bull whip." and settled about whittling the end of a broken branch.

Satisfied he had a fine point on it; he removed his boots, rolled up his pants legs and edged into the water. It was warm and the soft mud on the bottom of the creek squashed up between his toes. It felt good; he wiggled them and imagined it might draw the attention of the fish thinking his toes were worms. He waited for one to swim by. Feeling something brush against his leg he looked down thinking he would see a fish or two, but instead he saw a big water snake wrapping around his leg. With a blood-curdling yell he splashed and clambered from the water onto the bank, his heart pounding, had he been bitten? Was he to die of snakebite alone on this grassy bank?

With trembling fingers he examined his body for fang marks, finding none he sank to the ground in relief. How was he to catch a fish? He watched as his spear floated down the creek caught in the current of the slow moving water.

With a shake of his blond head he brushed away the leaves and debris he picked up while rolling on the ground. Reaching for his hat as he looked around he spotted wild grapevines growing in the trees nearby, "I guess that's breakfast." he told his horse who looked on with interest between nibbles of lush grass growing along the bank. Donning his boots and giving a wide berth to the snaky water he picked a hat full of the wild fruit.

Sitting in the shade of the big cotton wood he stuffed his mouth with the sour grapes spitting the seed toward the creek testing out his spittin' powers. He bet he could win a spitting contest. He had been practicing for some time to see how far the spittle would go. The grapes didn't taste like fried fish but it was better than nothing. Filling his pockets with what he didn't eat he saddled up and hit the trail.

The sun shone hot on his back burning through the thickness of his broadcloth shirt. He could feel his neck burning red. Shifting in his saddle and pulling his hat low he sought what shade he could muster up. He longed for a breeze; the day was hot and sultry. Tall trees lined the road on either side cutting off any wind that might manage to get through the thick foliage.

Plodding along wondering where he was going he spotted an animal lying in the ditch along the road. As he neared he could tell it was a big hairy dog. Was it dead? He got off his horse to take a closer look. He stood studying it for a few minutes before picking up a stick and squatting down beside it. He waited watching the hound intently. Was it breathing? Reaching out with the stick he poked at it. Suddenly the dog's eyes popped open and his tail gave a lazy wag. The surprise of it caused Carlo to fall back.

The dog raised his head. They sat there eyeing one another. Carlo looked around wondering if there was a house close by; his mind was still on how hungry he was. Maybe he could get something to eat, but after looking at the dog a second time decided he looked hungry himself.

Carlo didn't say anything; he just got back on his horse. The dog watched him and as he rode away got up, stretched and followed after them. Carlo kept watching for a house, that old dog had to belong to somebody.

Spotting an orchard and a peach tree loaded with ripe fruit Carlo climbed down from Tony's back. There was an old ramshackle house nearby, but from the looks of it no-one had been around in a long time, he supposed the peaches were for anyone who happened by. Climbing the fence he helped himself. He paid no attention as juice ran down his chin, they were mighty tasty. He ate til his stomach hurt, then picked some to take along. He didn't know how long he could live on fruit but it looked like that may be the way of it. Making a sack of his neckerchief by tying the corners together, he hooked the bag of peaches over his saddle horn.

'Dawg', as he decided to call the scroungy mutt trailing along with him, laid in the shade and watched. That appeared to be one lazy worthless dog Carlo thought. Heading down the road once again he noticed him following along, tongue out and head hanging low. He figured that mutt never got in much of a hurry over anything.

All at once a rabbit jumped from the brush. Tony shied away and Carlo grabbed for the saddle horn. Like a flash of lightening Dawg was on the rabbits trail. Startled, Tony kicked up his heels. "Whoa boy, whoa." Carlo pulled back on his reins and held on. "You're bout as ornery as Pa's old mule." He told the skittish horse.

Dawg had disappeared into the brush. Carlo figured he had seen the last of him when he appeared carrying the limp rabbit in his mouth. Carlo stopped and looked at him in amazement as he dropped the rabbit at Tony's feet and looking up wagged his tail. It sure looked to him like the dog was grinning.

Carlo piled off that horse in a split second and grabbed up that luscious hunk of meat. They were going to have a fine meal today, thanks to that worthless ole dog, who was suddenly Carlo's best friend.

Finding a good spot off the road Carlo unsaddled Tony and set about preparing the catch and setting up camp.

That pocket knife Pa gave him sure did come in handy and lucky for him he still had those matches he took from the back of the cook stove. He had only used one of them down behind the barn when he tried to smoke that grapevine. His friend Billy Rogers was nuts, that fire from the match sucked right through that hollow vine and burned his tongue. He wouldn't ever try that again.

After skinning and cleaning the Rabbit, he fashioned a spit and gathered twigs and small branches from the ground to build a fire in a nest of rocks, he turned the meat slowly watching it drip juice into the coals and brown til it was done on all sides. It sure was good eatin', and he shared it equal with Dawg and gave him the bones to gnaw on for desert while he ate a juicy peach.

As he ate he eyed the rabbit skin wondering what he could make of it. Seemed a shame to waste it, so he made a twig frame and stretched it as best he could, vowing to tan the hide and make a present for his Ma. He might go home for Christmas some day after he had traveled the world a bit.

Dawg moseyed over and lay down beside him; Carlo absently put his arm around his neck and pulled him in close. The two of them sat there by the creek gazing at the water as it foamed and gathered among the rocks, then washed away in swirls to disappear from sight.

Carlo dosed but woke with a start when he heard loud voices from the road overhead. Dawg was gone. Sensing danger Carlo quickly went to his horse and covered his nose to keep him quiet. He had chosen a place on the creek where a small wooden bridge passed over nearby. He knew they were hidden from sight from the main road and it should be a good place to camp for the night. His fire had burned down to ashes. Now he was glad of that.

He couldn't hear everything they were saying, but he could tell there was trouble. Seemed they were arguing and somebody was mad. All he could hope was that they didn't see him. He wished he knew what happened to Dawg.

He wondered if he might get on old Tony and ride quietly away, but there was no place to ride too, he was trapped down here as long as they were on the road above. Looking about for an escape route, other than the narrow path that led to where they were, he caught sight of Dawg coming along the edge of the creek. He hoped he wouldn't give them away.

He heard the sound of scuffling and a lot of grunting as a struggle took place and dirt was stirred up on the road above, there was a loud bang, it had to be a gunshot. Carlo flinched and Tony reared back dragging Carlo with him. Carlo held onto his reins for dear life hoping the folks above didn't see them below. All sound stopped, a deep voice cursed. Carlo held his breath and hoped the pounding of his heart could not be heard.

Dawg had stopped at the sound then came on the run, swift as the wind. Coming to a sliding halt next to Carlo he dropped another rabbit at his feet and looked up expectantly. Carlo put his hand out to rub his head, suddenly Dawg caught scent of the intruders, the stiff hair on his neck rose and a deep low growl sounded from his throat, Carlo grabbed him and pulled him close. Dawg strained to get away but Carlo held on.

He heard the creak of leather; a horse whinnied and stamped his feet, then the sound of horse hoofs pounded across the wooden bridge as it ran away.

Holding on to Dawg who was straining to climb the bank and investigate, Carlo waited and listened. Hearing nothing, he ventured up the path to the roadway, Dawg leading the way. When he reached the top, Dawg was sniffing at a body sprawled on the ground. Carlo had never seen a dead body before, especially someone who had been murdered and he wasn't sure he wanted to now. Assuming the man was dead Carlo jumped back in surprise when the man's arm reached out to Dawg. Carlo cautiously approached and looked down into the dark eyes of the wounded man.

"Help me." He whispered, then closed his eyes.

How was he to help the man he wondered, he was too big, there was no way he could lift him. He couldn't leave him lying on the road; it was a long way back to get help. If he could get him to that old house he had seen a ways back, maybe then he could go get his Pa.

What would Pa do, how would he handle the situation? He thought on it and decided he would make a traverse, he had watched his Pa build one many times to move things on the farm and had a fair idea how it was done. The horse could pull him back to the abandoned house, out of the sun and away from nosey animals. Carlo looked over his shoulder at the thought. There were probably wolves along this creek, or maybe even panthers.

Quickly searching among the trees for broken branches he found some the right length to build his frame. Taking out that handy pocket knife once again, he cut a length from his rope and weaving it through and around the tree limbs made a carrying rack to tote the injured man. Now the big problem was getting him onto it. He studied what to do. Taking his sleeping blanket he laid it beside the man, rolled him onto it, then dragged him over to it and rolled him onto the traverse. As he was about to tie it to old Tony, who was spooked and leery of the prone man on the ground and the smell of blood, a saddled horse appeared from the edge of the trees. Thinking it belonged to the wounded man he attached the rope to the horse's saddle, then remembering the rabbit Dawg had caught, he hurried down the path and grabbed it up thinking he might fix something to eat later. Climbing onto ole Tony and leading the buckskin he started for the 'peach orchard' house. It was slow going making sure the man didn't roll off the makeshift carrier.

When at last they pulled up to the abandoned farmhouse Carlo pushed the door open and went inside to see if it was fittin' to leave a man in while he went for help. The house had evidently been empty for a log time. A cotton stuffed mattress lay on the floor, half its stuffing torn out by wild critters. Carlo figured some hobo had stayed in the house before and bedded down by the fireplace.

Rolling his charge off the carrier onto the ground he proceeded to drag him inside, trying to ignore the moans of the man as he bumped him up the steps and across the threshold to the waiting mattress.

After seeing to his wound and dressing it as best he could, Carlo sat back to rest and study the man before him. He wasn't all that old and looked as though he was from the city. No-one he knew wore clothes like the ones this guy had on. And his shoes . . . or boots, they were fancy and shiny. Carlo couldn't help but wonder where he came from and where he was going.

Hearing his stomach growl reminded him he was hungry again. He better get that rabbit skinned 'fore it ruined. How glad he was to have rabbit twice in one day. He knew he was lucky that ole dog showed up when he did. He had considered calling him 'Worthless' but he could never do that now. He stole a look at the hairy critter and decided he was a right good-looking animal.

It was getting on toward dark and Carlo didn't take to the idea of traveling down that long road after the sun went down, so he decided to stay there and leave early in the morning, come daylight.

He hoped the fellow would hang on 'til he got help. Leading the two horses to a shed he had seen out back Carlo paid close attention when Dawg stopped and peered into the darkness of the building. After all they didn't know what happened to the shooter, was he still around? The hair didn't stand up on Dawg's back but Carlo felt like it did on his. It was plumb spooky out there.

He hurried to make sure the horses were secure and then started slowly back toward the house but glancing over his shoulder he felt sure someone was about to snatch him up and ran the last few steps slamming the door behind him. It hadn't helped his apprehension that Dawg had run past him and got into the house before he did. Big scare-dy cat! Some protector he was gonna be!

Carlo cleaned the rabbit and built a fire in the fireplace. Finding an old syrup bucket, he used it as a stool and watched as the rabbit cooked, its juices popped and spit as they hit the open flames. The odor of the roasting meat filled the little room and the glow from the fireplace cast shadows about the barren walls. It was spooky, but Carlo was mighty tired from all the activity. Making a hopeless attempt to feed the young man he and Dawg cleaned up every last bit of it, then snuggled in his blanket before the fire and fell into a deep sleep. He figured Dawg could handle the spooks.

He woke to the voice of the injured man calling out in a weak voice.

"Boy, do you have some water?"

Grabbing up his canteen, he hurried to the man's side, opened it and held it to his mouth. The man drank thirstily then fell back to the mattress.

"I'm going for my Pa. He'll help you."

"How far do you have to go? Will it be long?"

"He's in Portersville."

The young mans eyes widened and he whispered, "That's my home. My name is Sam Porter. The town is named for my grandfather."

Carlo studied him skeptically, then said, "You don't look like nobody I ever seen around here in them fancy cloths."

The boy gave a weak laugh. "I've been away at school for a long time." He closed his eyes and was very quiet, Carlo was afraid he had passed out when he whispered, "Go quickly and hurry. I am very weak."

Carlo jumped up grabbing his hat. "I'll be back quick as I can . . . Sam."

Sam opened his eyes and the corner of his mouth lifted in a smile. He waved as Carlo left the room.

Rushing to his horse he saddled up then turned to Dawg who was patiently waiting and said. "You Stay here Dawg and look after Sam. I'll be back."

Dawg's ears perked up and he cocked his head to one side, he wanted to go with Carlo but when he moved to follow, Carlo said again "Stay." Reluctantly he lay down on his stomach and watched him ride away.

Carlo liked the young man, even if he did sound different and wear weird looking cloths. He knew he better hurry and get him some help and he set off at a gallop.

He had been away from home for two nights and he figured he was in for a licking for running away but he would just have to take his licks if he was gonna help his new friend, Sam.

He hardly slowed down except to let Tony get a drink and cool down some. It was nearing suppertime when he rode through the gate to the farm. He saw his Pa walking from the barn to the house, so he was pretty sure Mama had supper ready.

He took off his hat and waving it went whooping and hollering down the road. Pa stopped and shading his eyes against the sun watched him ride in. Reining up, he slid to a halt in front of him and jumped down. He felt a thrill at seeing his Pa, even knowing he was in trouble.

Hat in hand he stood before him, "Pa . . ."

"Where ya been boy?" His voice was gruff, but he didn't sound mad, in fact Carlo thought he looked glad to see him.

"Pa, there's a boy back down the road a ways that's hurt real bad, he's been shot. He said Portersville is named after his grandpa. His name is Sam, I told him you would help him." He ended breathlessly, a question in his voice.

"Young Sam Porter? Where is he, boy?" He asked placing a warm hand on his shoulder and looking him square in the face, then without waiting for an answer turned back toward the barn, "How did you happen to find him?"

"I saw it all Pa." he said as he followed him into the gloom of the barn and grabbed up harnesses they needed to hitch a team to the wagon.

"Which way did you come? I'll head in that direction; you ride on into town, go to the Porter's house and roust them out, then follow after me and show us where he is." Climbing onto the wagon-seat he added, "Go tell your Mother you're home and where we're going, then get to town."

Carlo was mighty glad he was going in and could grab a handful of biscuits before he climbed back on Tony.

"Ma I'm home." He called coming into the kitchen. Ma almost dropped the gravy bowl. She sat it down and held out her arms, tears forming in her eyes. She pulled him close and held him. He was ashamed he made her cry. Turning him loose she stepped back and looked him up and down. "You alright Carlo?" she asked softly, he nodded.

"Why did you go and do a thing like that to your Pa? He has been sick with worry." She went on in a stern voice. "Just you wait young man, you are in trouble."

"Pa knows I'm here Ma, there's a boy hurt and Pa has gone to help him. I'm ta go get the Porters and take them along, it's their boy Sam."

"Sammie?" she asked in surprise.

How come everyone seemed to know who he was but himself, Carlo wondered. Grabbing up a chicken leg and a big fluffy biscuit he hurried from the kitchen.

"Tell Miz Porter I'll be right in, Carlo." She called after him as she took off her apron and reached for her hat. He climbed astride Tony and headed for Portersville.

It was only a mile into town and Carlo lost no time in getting there. He had never had reason to go to the Porters fine home on Cedar Hill. He hesitated at the gate seeing the imposing lion statues on either side of the front door. Gathering up his courage he walked boldly forward and rapped on the brass knocker. Expecting Mr. Porter to open the door, and knowing exactly what he was going to say, he was taken back when he looked into the blue eyes of a girl his own age. He stood there struck dumb. She was the prettiest girl he had ever seen in all his born days.

"Yes?" her voice was like a silver bell. He stared.

"Yes?" she asked for the second time. Coming to his senses he grabbed off his hat and swallowing hard he said with a swagger he didn't really feel, "I'm here to see Mr. Porter."

On hearing a voice in the background she turned calling out, "It's a boy to see you father." She stood aside and a large man stepped to the door.

Looking at first one and the other while twisting his hat in his hands he said, "It's your boy, Sam, he is hurt and my Pa has gone to help him and sent me for you." Mr. Porter just stood there looking at him.

"You're to come with me, quick like." He added.

"Who are you, and how do you know Sam?" He questioned.

"My name is Carlo Duncan. We live on Dobbins Road." he explained anxiously, "We got to hurry. My Pa took the wagon and we have to catch up. Sam got shot."

"Shot? Boy do you know what you are talking about?" the man said in shocked surprise. "What makes you think it was Sam?"

"He told me that was his name and that he was on his way home from school." Carlo worried; he never expected to be doubted by Sam's father.

Mr. Porter studied him; he seemed suddenly to decide he was telling the truth, much to Carlos relief. "I'll get my coat and hat." he said and turning found his young daughter standing there wringing her hands with tears in her eyes.

"Cindy, get your Mother while I saddle my horse," he said as he followed Carlo out the door. Carlo stopped, and looking at the girl said,

"Ma said tell your ma she would be here directly." He told the tearful girl. He saw Mr. Porter pause and look at him again, then nod his head.

Once on the road there was no chance for any conversation. Carlo worried ole Tony might be getting too tired to keep up the pace but the sturdy little horse seemed to get his second wind and had no problem keeping up with the big brown, Mr. Porter rode.

They soon caught up to Pa and he explained what Carlo had told him about finding Sam. At Pa's suggestion, when he discovered they still had a ways to go, Carlo tied Tony to the wagon and crawled onto it's bed and went to sleep thinking of Sam's blue-eyed sister. Her name is Cindy, he marveled. He sure hoped Sam was still alive.

The barking of a dog woke him. It was Dawg raising cane at the intruders coming near the house. Aside from Dawg, there was no sign of life, the house was dark. Carlos hopes sank. Carlo called out to Dawg as he growled and threatened Pa and Mr. Porter.

"Here Dawg." jumping from the wagon bed Carlo held out his arms. Dawg hesitated only briefly, then ran to him circling and jumping up. "Good boy. Settle down now." He roughed his hair and put his arms around him as he waited to see what they found inside.

"Carlo, pick up the blankets we're bringing him out." Pa called. Carlo watched as they came out, Sam's father carried him like a child and Pa, handing Carlo the lantern, placed the mattress in the wagon. Sam gave Carlo a wan smile as his Dad put him in the back and covered him with the quilts Pa had brought along. He was pale in the dim light and Carlo, relieved he was still alive, climbed in to ride along with him.

"Come on Dawg." he said motioning for the mutt to jump into the wagon.

"Whoa, whose dog is that?" Pa asked.

"He's my dog, Pa. Is it okay? Can I keep him?"

"We'll see." He said as he climbed into the wagon and started for Portersville, Mr. Porter riding close behind kept an eye on his boy. Dawg snuggled next to Carlo as they rocked and bounced down the rough road. Soon the motion lulled them both to sleep.

Next he knew they were stopping in front of Mr. Porters House. The eastern sky was showing light as Sam's Mother rushed out the door and down the steps with Carlos Mother close behind. To his disappointment Carlo didn't see anything of the blue-eyed sister. In a few minutes a darkfaced man went scurrying from the house and down the road after the doctor.

Carlo and Dawg stayed in the wagon. The doctor came back with the dark man in a buggy and hurried inside. Soon Pa and Ma came out and they headed out Dobbins road. He heard Pa telling Ma that Sam had been way-layed and robbed and if it hadn't been for Carlo and Dawg finding him he would have died alongside the road. Carlo had a glad feeling that warmed him through and through when thinking he saved Sam's life. Pulling into the yard at the house, Ma climbed down from the wagon.

"We got chores to do Boy." Pa sounded tired. Carlo figured he would do most of the work; it had been a long night.

Putting away the team and wagon Pa eyed Dawg. "If he messes with the chickens or the stock he'll have to go, understand that. He is you're responsibility." Having said that, Carlo figured he meant he could keep him for his own.

That afternoon the dark-skinned man Carlo had seen that morning come to the farm with a letter and gave it to Pa, then left. Pa studied it and handed it to Ma. It was really a letter for Carlo. They read it to him at suppertime.

Mr. Porter wanted to thank him for what he did for Sam and thanked Pa for being such a good friend and neighbor. He offered Carlo the opportunity to go to school with his son in the fall, all expenses paid. He hoped he would consider it, kinda like a reward for being nice and saving Sam's life. Carlo didn't think he had done all that much, but he would think on going to school. He liked the idea of being friends with Sam, which meant he could see Cindy sometimes.

All in all it had been quite an adventure, he had a dog now, had made a new friend, and met a pretty blue eyed girl, and to think he owed it all to Anna . . . and the pin.

He studied his sister across the supper table, 'Miss Uppity Anna' he called her to himself. He smiled, she looked up seeing him, she narrowed her eyes in suspicion.

He laughed. He was home.

© 2008 Bodrury

"Tumbleweeds"

Boone pushed the gate open and rode through into the barren yard leading to the ramshackle house. Wind gusts sent tumbleweeds skimming across the crusted dirt as he rode up to the porch. Squeaking windmill blades added to the forlorn feel of the place. It looked deserted except for the thin trail of smoke that rose from the chimney and vanished in the blue summer sky overhead.

Swinging down from the saddle, Boone froze when he heard the clicking of a rifle being cocked. He called out,

"My gosh, Josie, it's me, Boone."

He jumped when the rifle boomed and dirt kicked up at his heels. Grabbing the reins of his startled horse he attempted to calm him while keeping his eye on the rifle sticking through the open window.

"Welcome home Boone." Came a southern drawl from the doorway as a golden haired girl stepped onto the porch.

The ragged jeans and faded shirt she wore did little to hide the fullness of her young body, she was no longer the little girl he had left there three years before.

She stood there smiling before dashing across the space between them, throwing herself into his arms. He dropped the reins and held her as she smothered his face with girlish kisses.

"Boone." she cried," I thought you'd never come."

Disengaging himself from a tangle of arms and legs he sat her back on the porch holding her at arms length. Tears of happiness streaked down her face.

"I'm sorry it took so long Josie, your letter was a long time catching up to me."

Holding his hand she pulled him inside, suddenly overcome with shyness she dropped it. Looking at him she was at a loss of what to say or do. Wringing her hands she asked,

"Are ya hungry, I have beans and fried corn mush, it's fresh, I just cooked it?"

"Sounds good Josie."

She busied herself serving up a plate for him. Placing it on the table she sat down and watched, her elbows on the table and chin resting on the palm of her hands. He was hungry and meager though it was, it had a good flavor. Someone had taught Josie how to cook. He cleaned his plate and took seconds. When he was through he leaned back watching Josie as she cleaned up.

"How have you managed to get by since Ma and Pa died?" He asked as he rolled a cigarette. The place was run down but it was clean and neat and she seemed well fed. She sure wasn't thin anyhow.

"It wasn't easy. I had to sell off nearly everything to hang on for ya, but I did it Boone. It's free and clear. Not nothing owed against it." She said with pride.

"For me?" he asked in surprise as he struck a match under the wooden table and lit his smoke.

"Sure . . . Pa said to me before he died," she went on tears in her eyes, "Hang on til Boone gets here, it's all I got in the world to leave 'im. And I promised I would." A tear slid down her face. Boone didn't know what to say.

"You been here alone all this time?"

"Well who did ya thinks gonna be here with me?" she asked and waited for his answer. Boone didn't say anything so she continued,

"Pa said a mans only got three things that is important in this life, his word, his family, and his land. As long as ya got those you'll be okay, but without 'em it would be a powerful useless life. Never leave the land and you'll always have a home, he said, you can survive there."

Boone got up and walked to the door and looked out on the dried up farm. Pa scratched out a living here for years and what did it get him . . . a broken down body and a burying ground. That's not for me he thought. He turned back to Josie standing behind him, looking out across the yard.

"I buried 'em up yonder under the bodart tree. Ya wanta go pay your respects?" she asked softly," I'll wait here and let you have time alone with 'em."

Boone had not given any thought to where they were buried; his main concern after the initial shock was Josie. He had grieved and put it away, now he would say his goodbyes for Josie's sake, as well as his own. He walked slowly up the hill to the big tree where he had grown up playing. Many hours he had spent under this tree, dreaming of places he wanted to see and things he wanted to do. Being a farmer was not one of them. He squatted down looking at the simple headstones placed on the graves. Josie had engraved the words 'Mother' and 'Father' on them as well as their names, birth, and death dates. They were the only Mother and Father she ever had. He remembered the day Pa brought her home bundled up in a pink and blue quilt. He was so curious what was in there. He was five years old.

Her parents had been killed when their wagon had been attacked by Indians. Josie was the only survivor. No one knew who they were. Most of the families around had a houseful already so Pa brought her home to us, Ma and Me. That was eighteen years ago. Time had passed all too fast. He felt an ache in his heart for these two he loved so much. He had stayed away too long. He wondered if his Dad had needed him. He walked away, his vision blurred as he stumbled down the hill.

Josie watched from the porch. How she loved him. She didn't just hold the farm for him, she held herself for him, too. Ma had said, when he gets the wanderlust out of his system he'll be back, Josie girl. Just wait and see, he will come back to his roots.

"Where's that old mutt, Rascal?" he asked as he come up on the porch.

Josie laughed, "He has a girl friend over at the Turners place. Been gone for a few days courting. He'll be back, wore out and beat up by the competition, but he'll be okay. He knows where home is."

Boone sat down on the steps and reaching over picked up some pebbles from the ground and threw them one by one, skimming across the packed dirt.

Josie watched him from the porch bench.

"I guess we'll sell the place, get you settled in town."

"You can't do that." Josie cried jumping to her feet and looking down on him in amazement. "You can't be serious, this is our home."

"I'm not a farmer Josie. I'm not staying here, look what it did to the folks. It killed 'em and for what?"

"I can't believe you Boone. This place is a part of them, they loved it here. It meant everything to your Dad."

"Well not to me." he said emphatically, getting up and walking toward the barn.

Josie could not believe what he said. She looked around at her surroundings. He didn't see what she saw, the rains coming and the crops growing, a man and woman working side by side, children playing in the yard, loving one another, growing old together, just like Ma and Pa, she saw a home and security with the land. She was blinded by tears that filled her eyes and ran unchecked down her face. She would not let him do this. Somehow she had to hang on.

The afternoon turned into night and Josie lit the lamp. Boone didn't come back to the house. Josie climbed the ladder to her loft room and lay in the dark thinking of what was to come. She heard Boone come in and the light below went out. The night seemed endless.

With daylight she climbed down, stoked the fire and made coffee, then waited on the porch for Boone to wake up. She had a plan, she would buy the farm and he could go, and with him all her dreams. She fought the tears. She would never let him know her heart was broken. This was not the Boone she remembered.

The door opened and Boone stepped out, a cup in his hand. Seeing the dejected figure in the old rocker he said,

"I'm sorry Josie."

"I'll buy the farm from you." She stated quietly.

"With what?" he asked in surprise, "match sticks?"

Her eyes flashed as she looked up at him.

"I'll figure out a way. I am not giving up my home." she said heatedly.

Boone shook his head and leaned against the porch post. "You got no business out here by yourself."

"I managed for eighteen months, I'm sure I can manage the rest of my life, too."

Seeing the anger and pain on her face, Boone realized how serious she was.

"You don't have to buy it Josie, I'll sign it over to you. It belongs more to you than to me anyhow."

Josie turned away from him. She wanted to strike him and scream and throw things but knew it would be pointless. He didn't care about the farm or her. She said nothing, then heard him go back inside. When he came out he said,

"I am sorry you've had to manage on your own, Josie. I wrote out a bill of sale and I left you some money to help out for a while." He saw her shoulders stiffen as he talked. "I'm gonna hit the trail, I'll be in touch." He stepped off the porch. She spoke up,

"You're like tumbleweed, Boone. Ya broke loose and now you're going whichever way the wind blows. Getting nowhere, going nowhere, just like those tumbleweeds out there." She said sadly. "I love ya Boone and I've waited on you to come home. Whose gonna mourn you when you die on the trail. You'll lie in an unmarked grave and they will put nothing on your headstone. They'll never even know you passed through there on you're way to nowhere." Her voice choked as she talked.

Boone walked on to the barn and saddled up, tying his bedroll and pack behind the saddle. Mounting, he rode toward the gate. His gaze swept the farm and up the hill to the bodart tree and the headstones that marked the folks resting place. He remembered the loving glances they had for one another, the pride and the tenderness. He remembered, and then put it away with all the other memories of his past. He opened the gate and rode through and looked down the long trail ahead. As he shut the gate he heard her call out,

"Goodbye, Boone."

He looked back; she stood there a lonely golden haired girl watching him. She waved.

He turned and rode away. Where was he going? He thought of the things Josie had told him. Things his pa had said about family and the land. Josie was his family. She offered it all to him when she said she loved him. All he had to show for all his roaming was what he had tied to his saddle.

What was he afraid of? Turning out like his Pa? Thinking about it his Pa had everything. He worked hard, but he had a woman that loved him, a warm bed and someone to share it. He raised his food with his own hands and he was proud of what he had done with his life, of the legacy he was leaving for those he loved. And here he was walking away.

A tumbleweed blew across his path and bounced down the road before him going nowhere. Then veered to the left and caught in the fencerow with others of its kind.

Boone stopped and watched as it burrowed deeper into the mass. It'll take root, he thought.

He turned sideways in his saddle, hooked his leg over the horn and taking out the makings he rolled and lit a cigarette. He sat there, his horse stamping his feet, impatient to go. Boone looked down the endless road before him, then looked back the other way, from where he came.

He mashed out his smoke between his fingers and sat straight in his saddle, turning around he could see her still standing there looking after him. He sat there a minute then said,

"What the hell, even a tumbleweed has to stop someplace."

He spurred his horse to a gallop. He was going home.

"One Summer on Route 66"

The bug moved slowly across the dirt pushing and guiding the perfect ball he had created of manure gathered from the cowshed. Polly lying on her stomach on the splintered porch of the old farm house watched curiously. Wisps of golden hair flew around her oval face and her brown eyes watched intently as the bug traveled over the uneven ground, his spindly legs working continuously. What was he going to do with it she wondered, where was he going? He will never get there she thought.

Loosing interest she rolled over on her back and looked past the cover of the porch to the white billowing clouds gathering on the horizon. They were in constant motion, building and ebbing, rising here and falling there, going nowhere. It was the same with her she thought, going nowhere.

She could hear the traffic on the highway across the wheat field. Highway "66", some big shot guy in Oklahoma had named it, Pa said. Talk was they were gonna pave it soon. Right now there was a constant dust cloud hovering over it caused by the powdered rock and dirt that made up the surface. It had put a lot of folks to work busting up rock at the gravel pit to build the road. I 'spose it had been a good thing. They paid a dollar a day and that had fed a bunch of hungry folks around here, even Pa had done it for a while but now that pit was closed down and a lot of folks was out of work.

It was a busy road at night, you could see the car lights snaking across the country in the dark, Polly wondered about all those folks leaving their homes and making that long trip, where were they all going?

A bunch of 'em got lost or caught sight of the windmill and wandered past our old farm house. Most of 'em had hungry looking kids in the car and Mama always fed 'em something. It wasn't like we had a lot to eat ourselves but Mama always found something to share. She loved kids. Pa was always helping out with a little gas or fixing flats and filling up their canvas waterbags before sending them on their way. Our old windmill sure came in handy it seemed. It was a favorite with anyone that stopped by. Every vehicle that left had a dripping bagful of water tied to the front of their radiator.

Pa said he wasn't about to leave the farm. As long as he had it, we had a place to live, he wasn't sure those folks would when they got to where they were headed.

One of these days I'm gonna go down that road Polly thought to herself. Maybe to Amarillo or on even to New Mexico. Lots of folks that stopped by talked of going all the way to California. Now that the road was built, they said it went from one side of the world to the other, well at least all the way from one ocean to another. They said California was a golden opportunity, money to be made by the buckets full. She didn't know why her Pa didn't just jump at the chance; she would if she was old enough.

Clouds were building in the southwest, if it rained that old dirt road would be a muddy mess. Chances were some more folks might be stopping in; maybe even spend the night, maybe even more than that. She would be glad; it got mighty lonesome out here on this old farm in the summer. She liked to visit with all the families that laid overnight.

The county road grader crew stopped to get a drink from the well when they came by, when her Pa was around they would sit in the shade of the big elm by the well and visit a spell. Some of them would lay in the shade and take a nap. She heard them coming down the road, moving slow, stirring up the dirt as they came. This day there was a pickup truck following them. They stopped and piled down off the grader and out of the truck to come across the yard.

"Mornin' Missy." The man from the truck spoke, "Mind if we get a drink of that good water ya'll have here?"

Polly sat up and looked them over. They had someone new with them. A young boy, he had the bluest eyes she had ever seen. He had to be at least a head taller than she was and the dirt on his face did little to conceal his good looks.

She shook her head not saying anything as they continued on to the barrel of water. The boy hesitated. They looked each other over. Polly felt herself blush and looked away.

The men took down the tin cup that hung on a nail, skimmed the dirt off the water in the barrel and each one drank their fill. Sam, the one who drove the grader took his hat off and poured a dipper of water over his head cooling down. It was hot and dirty work. Polly watched.

The man who had spoken earlier smiled, took off his hat, and looking at Polly said,

"This here's my nephew, Chip, gonna be helping Sam out this summer on the roads. Learning the trade. He will be stopping by from time to time." Wiping the sweat from his forehead he put his hat back on. "Thanks for the drink, Missy." and started for the truck.

"My names Polly." she said, looking at the boy. He nodded and followed his uncle.

Sam wiped his face with a big red bandana and smiled at Polly.

"See ya next time, Polly."

Polly, her eyes following them, never moved from her spot on the porch. The boy looked back as they drove away and raised his hand in a wave unseen by the others.

Leaning back on the porch and looking up at the clouds she smiled. Maybe it wouldn't be such a bad summer after all. Guess she would wait about traveling down route 66 for a while.

Remembering the bug Polly sat up and looked to see how far he had traveled. He was almost to the fence. He had gone at least three ft. He might get there after all, where ever that was.

© 2007 Bo Drury

Pier 19

Watching the early morning sunlight sparkling on the water of the bay, Victor stood on the balcony of the high rise hotel. The roar from the waves was continuous as they rolled in, capping high, then died out along the sandy shore. A tanker was being towed out to sea by a small tugboat. He smiled as the miniature boat manipulated the giant ship easily through the waters.

He gazed absently beyond the breakers, watching the shrimpers in the bay, and thought of the dream he had the night before. It had something to do with Pier 19. He had dreamed a lot recently, although he couldn't remember them in their entirety, only bits and pieces. He mused thoughtfully over the dream and the events of the past few weeks.

Pulling a tightly rolled cigar from his breast pocket he held it to his nostrils savoring the aroma of the sweet smelling tobacco. Biting off the tip he spat it out and watched as it spiraled to the rocks below. Lighting it with small puffs he observed the smoke as it lifted, caught by the breeze from the bay and disappeared into nothingness.

Pier 19 had come to mind several times in the past few days, leaving him with a vague uneasiness each time. It was a strong feeling, a hunch, but he knew he had to go there, just as he had been compelled to come to Galveston. He learned long years ago to follow his hunches and so far, luck seemed to be with him.

He was a gambler; his life was a game of chance, he dared where no one else would. He knew he was a handsome man and his devil-may-care attitude and ready smile had carried him far. Few saw the dark-side beneath the pleasant relaxed appearance; the periods of unexplained depression and brooding. Staying active was the only way to fight the gloom that was his constant companion.

Hearing the water of the shower turn off, Victor's thoughts turned to Claire and the good fortune that brought them together. He flicked the cigar over the banister and entered the room. She came in clad only in a large towel. She was the best thing that ever happened to him. Toweling off quickly she pulled on the baggy white slacks and a loose long-sleeved shirt she had chosen as her beach clothes. She was sunshine for him; the sight of her lifted his spirits. He stood behind her as she brushed her long blonde hair, twisting it into a loop and holding it with a jeweled beret he had given her. Reaching for a red silk scarf for her neck she saw him shake his head. He hated the color red. She put it back and smiled into the mirror. Placing his hands on her shoulders he bent to press his lips to the nape of her neck. He loved the clean soapy smell of her skin. He looked up to see her watching him in the mirror. She smiled a seductive lazy smile, her sea-green eyes full of promise. As he studied her face the smile faded, replaced with a puzzled expression, "What's wrong, Victor?"

She was different from all the other women he had known. He was drawn to the sloe-eyed, dark haired women he met, until Claire came into his life.

He had been having a run of bad luck at the tables in Vegas when she sat down beside him. A fresh scent like summer rain caught his attention; he turned to discover her at his side. She glanced up and smiled. His luck changed. He shut down the table and moved to another, she went along. He asked her to go with him, she did. From that time on she had been by his side. He did nothing without her.

Pulling her up from her chair he slipped his arms around her. Sliding his hands beneath her loose blouse, he ran his hands over the smooth skin of her back and held her close. Covering her mouth with his own, he closed his eyes; the dream came back to him. He pulled back looking into her face, her dark lashes shaded her eyes, but he could see the question there. He told her about the dream and the need to search it out before they headed back to Vegas.

He had been waiting and watching for whatever it was he was supposed to discover in Galveston. They had been here more than a week and so far nothing had happened. In the beginning he had thought what he was looking for would be found along the beaches and had scavenged the shoreline intently, but after a few days decided he should look elsewhere. He studied everything he passed carefully, objects, places, and faces. He knew something was here all he had to do was find it.

Claire had fallen right into the role of a beachcomber, loving every moment of it, prowling the beach for her found treasures, oblivious of the trash washed up along the shore and black tar-balls that ruined her shoes the first day out. She swathed herself in lotions and covered her fair skin with sheer long sleeves and white loose-legged slacks, donned her wide brimmed hat and prowled the shell strewn sands filling her catchall with the tiny objects and colorful shells she discovered with the delight of a small child. Victor found no pleasure in the beach himself only the watching of Claire and the pleasure she took in her simple excursions along the beachfront.

When victor confided his dream of Pier 19 to her she was excited and willing to give up her day on the beach for a new adventure, eager to discover what waited for them on Pier 19.

During the few years they had been together she had learned to respect Victor's hunches. Rushing through breakfast they stopped by the hotel desk and asked directions to Ferry Road and Waterfront Street. Taking the city map offered to them they were on their way. Caught up in an adventuress spirit Claire could barley contain her excitement as they headed for the dock area, reading the street signs and laughing in anticipation?

Once they turned onto the street running parallel with the waterfront Victor slowed, almost coming to a stop.

"I have a bad feeling about this, maybe we should let it go, go on back to the hotel and spend our last day here on the beach." he said uneasily.

"No, this is more fun. It's like going on a treasure hunt." She said as she studied the map. Then exclaimed, "Oh no! There is no Pier 19! It jumps from 18 to 20. It skips 19!" She said in disappointment sinking back in her seat.

"Are you sure?" He asked in disbelief, at the same time turning where 19 should be. There before them was a long building of weathered gray wood. It had sparkling clean windows across the front and several newly painted signs reading "Restaurant", "Oyster Bar", and "Fish Market"

They parked and sat quietly in front of the building. Claire's disappointment was evident, but Victor felt somehow relieved. They each studied the surroundings carefully. Looking up Claire spotted a small sign at the back of the building above the roof.

"Look!" she cried in delight, "It says Pier 19. Let's go in." she opened her door jumping out excitedly.

Victor hesitated, then slowly got out and stood by the car looking at the small sign barely visible above the building. Again a feeling of foreboding came over him. A fleeting thought of another time, another place, a vague memory he was unable to grasp crossed his mind.

With reluctance he walked toward the entrance following Claire who had quickly gone ahead and stood waiting. She turned laughing and teasing.

"Come on Victor! Maybe you were here in another lifetime. This may have been a pirate's cove where they shanghaied men and sent them out to sea."

Victor laughed trying to shake the feeling of dread as he held the door for Claire, then stepped inside.

It was pleasantly cool. The aroma of fresh brewed coffee met them as they entered. The salad bar was piled high and fresh oysters lay in open shells on ice. The desserts were lined up to tempt all who passed and the employees were busy preparing for the noon rush.

Victor looked carefully around the room missing nothing. Old photos, signs, shells and stuffed fish adorned the interior; there was nothing out of the ordinary. The dining room faced out on the water and shrimp boats were moored at the docks. It was very scenic. Nothing made a connection with Victor. Claire giggled nervously as they got some of the hot coffee and made their way into the dining area to sit at the windows and watch the boats and their crews at work, still searching with their eyes wondering if there was something of significance there that they were missing, not wanting to overlook anything.

They sat not speaking, each lost in thought as they watched the sea gulls swoop in and out among the boats. Victor watched as a young oriental woman hurried down the walkway and out onto a ramp. The sunlight glistened on her dark hair. She glanced anxiously about; her dark eyes looked directly through the window and into—Victors. She hesitated as her almond eyes held his. He felt a shock soar through his body followed by a sudden unexplainable chill.

A dark haired man came up from the stairwell of one of the boats and called to her. She lowered her head, breaking the eye contact and turned her attention to the dark sailor. They appeared to argue. She looked once more in Victor's direction to find him still watching her before disappearing into the depths of the moored boat.

Victor found oriental women fascinating. There was an aura of mystic about them, a sense of danger he could not define nor resist. He had invariably been drawn to them, until he met Claire.

He jumped in surprise when Claire spoke, breaking into his thoughts.

"I love it down here, it is so beautiful and peaceful." She said as she watched the birds sweep down to feed from the water, their white wings spread in graceful motion.

"I'd like to go out on one of the boats; can we stay over another day and go out into the bay?" She smiled as she reached for his hand across the table, then not waiting for an answer turned back to watch the men along the docks working on their nets and fishing equipment.

"Let's go out and look around." She said standing and moving toward the exit door.

"Claire, this is a rough neighborhood, it's not for tourists." He answered.

"It's broad daylight. What could happen in the middle of the day?" continuing on to the bright red door.

Suddenly he remembered the dream. There had been a red door marked "Danger". He reached out calling, "Claire, Wait . . ."

She had already opened the door and stepped out. He rushed out behind her, clammy with sweat, his heart pounding.

She stood there in the sunshine, no one else in sight. He looked quickly around, certain there was some dangerous force nearby. There was nothing.

The seagulls continued to sweep in and out among the boats rocking gracefully as the water moved in gentle swells. Oyster shells littered the ground and were piled deep against the gray building. Quite different from the picturesque setting observed from inside and the pleasant odor of the savory food waiting there. Outside an unpleasant stench from bait and decaying fish hung in the air. Claire wrinkled her nose and looked down into the murky water where trash floated against the dock.

"I guess it's not so pretty out here . . ." she began when they heard a scream and looking up they saw the girl from earlier clamor topside of the boat and leap to the dock falling to her knees. Scrambling to her feet she rushed toward Claire and Victor. A look of terror on her face. The sailor followed her a large pistol in his hand, yelling. He stopped and aimed as the girl ran toward them.

Claire seemed frozen to the spot, unable to move though Victor called to her, hesitating only a second he lunged to the side knocking Claire to the ground. He heard an explosion the same time something hit him. The shock was similar to the one he felt as he looked into the dark eyes of the woman earlier. It jerked his body and slammed him to the ground. The pain was severe then he felt numbness spread over him. He heard Claire scream his name, another shot and someone fell next to him. "No!" he wanted to say "not Claire!" but no sound came from his mouth.

There was shouting and the sound of feet running on the oyster shells. Claire leaned over him lifting his head. There was blood on her white shirt . . . red on white! He turned his head to see who lay beside him, it was the girl, she reached for him as her almond eyes dulled and closed, her hand dropped.

Was it a dream? Why did he remember this from before? Not again, he cried.

Claire cradled him in her arms, disbelieving, as his eyes closed and his blood spilled out mixing with dark red stains left long years before . . . when his luck ran out on Pier 19.

© Bodrury 2009

"The Run"

The stifling heat, odor of horse-flesh and dust stirred up by the hundreds of humans and animals milling around was overpowering. Lizzie pulled her scarf over her nose while griping the reins in her hand as her horse stomped his hoofs impatiently. She dared not let go. Looping the lead rope around her left hand once more, making sure it was secure, she scanned the folks to her left looking for a familiar face. There he was, Carl, sitting loose in the saddle as though he were completely relaxed. How can he do that? Their eyes met, he winked and smiled. Lizzie was so tense she could feel the muscles draw taunt in her neck and shoulders. The camaraderie of the crowd had vanished as they had lined up waiting for the signal. Every person there was intent on reaching their goal before someone else beat them to it. The promise of free land in the Oklahoma Indian Territory had drawn folks from all over the world. Lizzie had met many of them but had no idea who her neighbors would be when this day was over.

The boom of a gunshot sent a sharp sensation surging through her body; she jerked and grabbed at the lead rope, fearing the frisky horses already straining for freedom would try to bolt. Some others on the starting line started forward before realizing it was not the signal to go, but 'sooners' being warned to hold up. Her horse strained at his bit, he was ready, the long wait and suspense was telling on all of them, man and animal alike. She tried to smile in return but it was forced. Carl had given her the responsibility of the horses. They were their grub stake; all they had other than the few belongings in the wagon alongside her. She looked at the old man in the drivers' seat of the buckboard. Would he be able to handle the team and get to the designated spot in one piece? She couldn't help but worry about the precious cargo he hauled. All of Carl's tools, everything she had to set up housekeeping, to furnish her new home, her wedding gifts. The old man pulled a pocket watch from his shirt, checking the hour. He glanced up at her and nodded as he put it away and picked up the reins. Carl had been watching also and when she looked toward him he gave a quick nod and settled in his seat, prepared to ride.

Lizzie felt a tingle of excitement course through her body. She pressed her knees to the saddle and leaned forward holding her breath, the very air around her charged in anticipation of the coming event, the run into no-mans land, the strip that promised each of them a new beginning, their future.

The signal sounded. Their wagon shot forward with a snap of a whip and a blood curdling yell from the old man along with a tremendous roar up and down the line as the mob surged forward. The startled horses in her charge pulled at the ropes rearing back and pulling loose from her hold leaving burns along her arm. Ignoring the pain, she fought to grab the ropes while struggling to control her own mount, but the horses, loose, tore in after the mass of riders and wagons moving forward hell-bent on reaching the plot of land they had chosen and were soon out of sight, lost in a cloud of dust.

It seemed the whole world had gone mad as they made the wild rush, Lizzie among them, searching frantically for the horses left in her care. She had no control as she moved with the crowd avoiding disasters that confronted her as wagons over turned, horses stumbled and fell, and uneven ground forced her to hold on for dear life. Bits of dirt and debris stung her bare skin as it was kicked up by the horses and spinning wheels of the wagons, tears blurred her vision as the wind whipped around her face.

Trying to stay in control of the run-a-way horse she rode was pointless; she gave the sure footed animal its head and prayed it would see her safely through the melee around her. She could think of nothing but trying to stay in the saddle. She would have to wait until the crowd thinned and the horse ran himself to exhaustion to go back and look for the ones Carl had left with her.

Far into the strip, on what had seemed an unending perilous ride, her horse slowed to a steady gait. Thoroughly shaken and upset over her loss and fearing the disappointment Carl would feel at her being unable to handle the job he had given her, she reined in the exhausted mare and slid from the saddle. Standing on a knoll she looked in all directions hoping to spot any thing familiar. She felt the hot sting of unshed tears as they formed in her dark eyes. She had no idea where she was or where she might find Carl. Was he safe? She had seen many fallen riders and overturned wagons, their contents scattered and trampled. Were hers among them? Pushing back her dark hair she realized it had fallen loose and her combs and pens were gone. Her new hat was hanging around her neck by the chin strap or it would have gone the way of the pens. She brushed at the dust on her riding habit and tying her hair back with her neck scarf climbed back in the saddle.

She had to find the horses; there was no time for tears now.

Picking a path through the rough terrain Lizzie wondered how they made it to where they were without breaking their necks.

In every direction there were folks walking, broken wagons and families who had overturned and now sat dejected and disillusioned about the run they had just attempted, Some were driving in their claim-stakes where they sat, giving up the notion of moving any further. Some eyed her fearfully; afraid she might be a threat. She waved and kept moving, alert always to the animals around her wondering if someone had laid a claim on her herd.

Suddenly a bearded man leapt from the nearby brush and grabbed at her reins, frightened and surprised she slid to one side avoiding his grasp. Her horse shied away and she reached for her quirt to use as protection should anyone else attempt the same thing.

"Oh, Carl." she whispered and fought back the urge to cry. It had never occurred to her she might be in danger, a woman alone in unfamiliar territory. From that moment on she only approached groups where other women could be seen and even then avoided most of them. Nowhere did she see any evidence of her horses.

Daylight began to fade as the sun dropped low in the west, and as night approached a chill filled the air. Lizzie had on her riding clothes with a long sleeved blouse but no jacket. The day had been warm and there had not been a need for one. She carried no bedroll, which was usual equipment when traveling, but there had been no need for that for the plan had been to meet and set up camp together, the 'old man', Carl and his partner, Tom Mingis.

The older man was Tom's uncle, or she assumed he was, and the only name she had ever heard him called was 'Ole Man', but she had noticed he could hold his own when it came to work. Now as she rode along in the dusk of the evening she wondered what his real name was. Would she ever see him again? She would love to about now and have a cup of that awful coffee he made, bitter and strong, but at least it would be hot and maybe warm her hands. They were numb from the cold and the tight grip she had kept on the reins all day made them stiff and ache. She was freezing cold and her teeth were chattering.

Shivering she pulled her arms close to her body hoping to find warmth. She had to stop before it got much darker, she could never find the horses in the dark and realized it was dangerous to ride on, not knowing or being able to see what was out there.

She thought again of the bearded man reaching for her. Would he have hurt her or was he only after her horse? She shivered again, but not from the cold.

Searching for a safe haven she found a little hollow among the cover of some young trees and dismounted. Unsaddling her horse she chose a spot to place the saddle and blanket backed by a large tree where she would feel safe and able to watch the open area for any movement. There was plenty of firewood on the ground if she had a way to build a fire but that was a bad idea as it could draw unwelcome visitors to her camp.

Securing her horse to a branch she rubbed him down with a handful of dry leaves while murmuring to him in a soothing voice. With a pat and promise of food later she sat down on the horse blanket, it was damp and smelled of a horse. Using her hat for a pillow she lay back against the saddle and pulled part of the blanket over her, right now it didn't matter what it smelled of, it was warm.

She thought of Carl and tears slid down her cheeks. Caught up in her distress she was oblivious to the sounds of the night around her. Where was he, was he okay? Was he looking for her, would he ever find her? She was lost, she sobbed in the dark, longing for the comfort of his arms. The horse turned a curious ear to the sound, all else was silent.

Waking with a start she opened her eyes to find a maize of tree branches hanging overhead. Momentarily confused about her whereabouts she sat bolt upright, then remembered the events of the previous day.

But wait . . . She listened intently, voices . . . none familiar, and the sound of a wagon passing over hard ground nearby. Her first impulse was to call out but remembering the man from the day before and knowing she was at a disadvantage on foot, and could be trapped in the small glen she had chosen for safety, she remained cautious. Rising quickly she hurried to her horse and covered his muzzle, stroking him gently to keep him quiet until she was certain the wagon had passed by and was out of hearing.

Feeling it was safe she quickly gathered the saddle blanket shaking away the dirt and leaves and prepared to saddle up. Her body ached from the wild ride and the night on the hard ground. Her mouth was dry and she craved food and water. Not sure her five foot of height and small frame had the power and strength to lift the heavy saddle onto the little filly's back she made an attempt to hoist it in the air as Carl had done. The attempt failed. With gritted teeth, and determination her second try got it high enough she could shove it the rest of the way. Now all she had to do was cinch it tight enough to stay and not slide off. Rosie, as she sometimes called the little mare, was guilty of puffing up to keep the cinch strap from being to tight. Giving her a poke in the flank make her deflate, toss her head and give Lizzie a resentful look.

"I know you're hungry and thirsty as I am, so let's go find those darn horses and something to eat."

Hamstrung by her long riding skirt she searched for a fallen log to assist her and was soon astride the horse.

"Ladylike or not, next time I'm wearing britches." She vowed.

Emerging from the thick stand of trees she looked in each direction deciding which way to go. They needed to find some water first, then look for the horses. She was determined to find them before she found Carl. She feared he would hate her for losing them. She thought of the trust he had put in her, his new bride. This was their honeymoon, their start on a life together. He would probably send her packing, back to Kansas!

How humiliating that would be, to face her Mother. She could see her now with that "I told you so look" on her face. She had been angry when Lizzie left with Carl. She hated him and would be delighted if he failed and Lizzie had to come back home. That was not going to happen! She would show her mother and Carl she had what it took to be a wife and helpmate. They would succeed the two of them together!

She turned in the opposite direction from where the wagon tracks led, back the way she had come. The horses had to be there someplace and she would find them.

This was nothing like Kansas she decided as she rode. There were boulders and short scrubby trees everywhere, hundreds of places for the horses to be hidden from sight. What would anyone want with this country? There was no farm land to be found here, she thought as she worked her way in and out of the hills and stands of tall trees and gully's cutting away the soil through the countryside. Coming upon a stream of running water almost hidden from sight in a mass of growth she and Rosie drank their fill and rested in the shade before Lizzie filled her canvas waterbag and moved on. They rode out of the wooded area onto low rolling hills covered in grass looking like waves on the sea swaying in the wind. It was beautiful.

The soil looked rich and fertile. Claim stakes had been driven into the ground. Could this be our place she wondered but then happened upon a wagon and campsite and found herself staring into the muzzle of a shotgun held by a nervous young man not more than thirteen or fourteen years old. Seeing she was a woman alone he lowered the gun, but eyed her suspiciously and looked past her to see if anyone followed.

"I'm alone," she said adding, "and lost."

He looked uneasy and at a loss as what to do.

"May I get down? I'm hungry. I lost my horses yesterday and have been searching for them." she went on explaining as she scanned the area assuring herself no one else was pointing a gun in her direction.

"My folks are gone . . . . to file on our claim." He replied gruffly. "They left me here to watch the place and run off claim jumpers." He raised the gun in her direction, and then lowered it again. Lizzie could see he was very nervous and that was frightening. He might just decide to shoot.

Still on her horse she went on with her explanation," I got separated from my husband. I'm sure he is looking for me. I've been out all night. Do you have something I could eat? I can pay you when my husband comes for me."

The young boy studied on that, looking at her he could see she was young, probably not much older than he was and right pretty, but his paw had warned him against anyone coming into the camp, it could be a trick.

"I will give ya sometin' to eat but stay in the saddle and don't try and pull any funny stuff 'cause I will shoot ya." He threatened as he backed over to the wagon and uncovered a pan of biscuits never taking his eyes from her. Taking a couple out he came as close as he dared.

"Think ya can catch these." She nodded and he tossed them one at a time toward her.

Taking a bite of the cold dry biscuit she nodded and swallowed hard then cautiously reached for her water bag, careful not to alarm him, she didn't want him thinking she was reaching for a weapon. Taking a drink and finishing the biscuit she gave him a small smile saying "Thank you." She put the other biscuit in her pocket and asked," What's your name? We might be neighbors." when he didn't answer she gathered the reins in her hand and backed away saying as she did," I'll ride on now." With a shake of her head she told him," You have nothing to fear from me. Good luck to you and your folks."

As she rode away he called after her,

"My names Charlie . . . Charlie Whatley."

She turned, gave a quick wave and spurred Rosie forward, anxious to put some space between her and the gun toting young man.

The sun came up hot beaming down. She had still seen nothing of her horses or Carl. She avoiding riding into any campsites she spotted but searched the stock around them for her familiar brood.

Coming onto a pool of water she decided to let Rosie rest and graze a bit while she bathed her face and arms in an attempt to cool down. Looking around, assuring herself she was alone, she removed her hat and long sleeved shirt and splashed the cool liquid onto her face and neck letting it run down her breasts and wet her bodice then sought the shade of a nearby tree and leaned back to rest a minute before climbing back in the saddle. Remembering the biscuit in her pocket she broke it in half and ate. She was beginning to feel desperate about finding their own camp site. Surely Carl was looking for her, but was she moving away from him? It was a big territory.

Feeling a sudden urgency to move on she donned her hat and blouse and reached for Rosie's reins. Rosie backed away tossing her head. Reaching out again, the horse shied away. Hot and tired and losing patience she lunged forward and stepped on the trailing reins then stooped to pick them up.

A warning rattle sounded nearby. She froze. Where was it? She was afraid to move. She tried to look around with out moving, she couldn't find it on the ground anywhere. It sounded again. Her heart pounded, it was close. She looked up. There it was, at eye level with her face on a boulder before her, coiled and ready to strike. It couldn't miss. The brief thought of dying alone out here of snake bite chilled her to the bone. Her adrenalin surged, in reflex she threw her self to the side rolling in the dirt just as the huge rattler launched his diamond back through the air. Missing his mark he slithered away into the brush. Lizzie lay there trembling, realizing how close she came to a sure death, she began to cry and laugh in relief.

To heck with the horses, she just wanted Carl. On shaky legs she gathered the reins and climbed onto Rosie's back unaware of the dirt and mud that covered her tear streaked face and damp cloths. Skirting the water she headed in the direction where she thought they started. She wanted to find Carl before the day ended; she didn't want to spend another night alone.

Moving at a brisk trot she rode over a rise and looked down in a small valley. There on the other side of a small creek bed a herd of horses bunched together that looked familiar. Where they hers? She couldn't believe it. Picking her way down the incline she spurred Rosie to a gallop, they were her horses, how did they end up together? Were they all there? It didn't matter, the biggest part of them were. Not taking time to study the embankment Lizzie plunged down into the water. The horse stumbled, floundered trying to get her footing; the more she struggled the deeper she sank into the mud below the surface. She was mired down.

Frightened, Lizzie fought to keep the horses head above the water, how deep could they go. Rosie stopped struggling. Lizzie could see they had stabilized, but how was she going to get out of the mire herself? In her struggle to get a footing Rosie had moved to the center of the creek bed and into deep water. Unsure of what would happen if she left the saddle, Lizzie stayed where she was the dark water swirling around her. How could this be happening, she was in sight of her goal, finding the horses and now unable to reach them.

What if no one came along, she would have to try and swim through the water and not get trapped in the muck below, but she had never learned to swim, and Rosie, she had to get her out of there too. Fortunately with the sun glaring down during the hottest part of the day she was in the shade of a cottonwood tree growing along the waters edge.

Lizzie hung her head, slumping in the saddle, she felt abandoned and lost, so sad she couldn't even cry. She was alone but for Rosie, the insects skimming the water and an occasional bird swooping through the tree tops.

"Hey lady, how long are you gonna sit there like that?"

Lizzie's head jerked up and she spun around at the familiar voice.

"Carl." she looked into his smiling face seeing relief there. He asked,

"Woman, where in tarnation have you been?"

She saw the Ole Man and Tom riding up behind him.

"We've been scouring the country side for you but all we could find were the horses." He said as he began to form a loop with his rope. "I'm going to toss the rope to you, Lizzie, grab hold and I'll pull you through the water. Hang on tight."

The rope fell short and he had to pull it in and try again. This time she grabbed it.

"Slide it over your head and under your arms. I don't want to have to wade out there and get you; I might get my boots wet." He laughed. How could he do that? Laugh after all she had been through?

Lizzie couldn't stop the flow of tears as she struggled with the wet rope, securing it to her waist she slid off Rosie's back into the water.

Once free of Lizzie's weight Rosie began to fight again to free herself of the soft bottom she had sunk into.

"Try to keep your head up out of the water." he called as she skimmed over the muddy surface toward him. He jumped from his horse tossing the rope to Tom and ran to the bank to pull her free of the mud. Wrapping his arms around her he held her close then pulled back to study her face cupping it between his strong hands.

"Are you alright?" he asked softly looking into her teary eyes.

"Yes," she whispered. "I am now." As she wrapped her arms tightly around him thinking she would never let go.

Helping her to her feet she caught the concerned look on the ole mans face standing behind them. He coughed and swiped his hand across his face wiping away the moisture on his weathered cheeks, then clearing his throat when he caught her eye said, "Welcome home Missy, I have some of that coffee you like waiting at the camp."

Lizzie laughed through her tears. "That sounds good, Ole Man."

© Bodrury 2009

"Ole Bob"

Old Bob just showed up one day. Come walking up into the yard from the dusty road and got his self a drink out of our horse tank, then laid down in the shade of the big elm tree by the windmill and stayed. When we came near him he just rolled those big soulful eyes at us and wagged his tail.

Pa took one look at him and said to us kids, "Don't go and get attached to him, if he's a egg-sucker or messes with the chickens he's gotta go."

He was a sorry looking dog, short, dirty-white hair with a big brown spot over his left eye. He wasn't a big dog, kinda mid sized and stout. We figured someone just dumped him along side the road like so many city folks do when they got tired of feeding him.

He was good natured, too lazy to do much else we thought. He didn't bother anything or anybody. Ma fed him the scraps from the table and he was happy with that. He followed us kids around while we did our chores and now and then he would chase a rabbit. He never got too excited over anything. He loved all the kids though, you could tell. Even Ma got attached to him.

Our little Sis was just a toddler. She could crawl all over him and he never moved or made a sound. If he got tired of being wallered on he would move to another corner of the room and flop back down.

He watched for the school bus everyday and met us at the cross-road and walked us home. Seemed he always knew what time it was, time to eat and time for the bus. We thought he was a pretty smart dog. Bad thing was, Pa never took up with him. He thought he was worthless. If we hadn't all been so crazy about him, Pa would have run him off.

Now we had a big old sow with a bunch of piglets. She was huge and mean. She took to killing chickens and eating 'em. Ma was some mad about it and told Dad he had to fix the fence so the ole pig couldn't get to the chickens any more. Those were her prize laying hens.

Pa set to fixing the fence but he needed some help. He came to the house and got Ma. Sis was asleep on the floor. Ma figured she would be alright with old Bob laying there beside her, so she took off her apron, hung it up, and went out with Pa. As she left she said to Old Bob, "You mind the baby, Bob. Don't let her out of the house now." And shut the screen behind her.

They hadn't been out long when the old bloodthirsty sow broke down the fence and got loose in the yard between the house and the barn. Pa saw she was out and cussed. Ma was scared she was going after the chickens. The sow headed in the direction of the house away from where Ma and Pa were working.

Ma looked toward the house to see Sis come toddling out. The sow spotted her about the same time. Guess the sow thought she looked like one of them fat chickens. Ma screamed, there was no way they could reach her before the sow did. Pa took off running. The sow was closing in on Sis who was happily running across the distance toward her.

Out of the house, screen door banging, came old Bob. He came tearing across the yard passing by Sis and took a giant leap. Bob grabbed the sow by the nose and rolled her, then went for her throat and tore it open. Pa got his gun and shot the old critter. That sow must have weighted in at six hundred pounds and Bob couldn't have weighed more than sixty.

Now you can bet Pa took a liking to Old Bob. We sure did eat good for a while too. Pork chops, bacon, sausage and the like. Those little piglets grew up just fine with out a Mama. And Old Bob had a home for life and a bed right by the fireplace.

© 2007 Bo Drury

A 'Whopper' of a Tale with Adelle

A soft breeze from the open window lifted and ruffled the papers strewn about the desks as the young students tried to focus their attention on the lesson in progress, a nearly impossible task.

Adelle gazed out on the lush green of spring as she grabbed her work and held it in place. It was the English class and they were reading from Ivanhoe. She was aware Anita had finished reading her paragraph and had taken her seat but her mind had been elsewhere and she had missed part of the story and lost her place.

"Adelle, continue." came Mrs. Sutton's soft voice from the front of the room.

Adelle didn't answer, why would anyone name their child Adelle, she wondered thinking of the many names she had rather be called.

The teacher looked up and searched for the young lady she had called on.

"Adelle?"

Still she ignored her.

"Adelle Dennis."

She pretended not to hear. She heard the rustle of movement and felt her classmates turn to look at her. She continued to gaze out the window observing a yellow butterfly flit from limb to limb.

Smelling the heavy fragrance of perfume old folks tend to wear and sensing a warm presence standing beside her she sat very still, barely breathing, wondering if she was about to get a thump on her head.

Turning slowly from the window she looked directly into a set of pearl buttons bound tightly to a full bosom. Her gaze slowly traveled the distance from the mound of flesh to the crepe folds of a sagging throat, past a quivering chin and pursed lips and into the blue eyes of a very impatient teacher.

"Do you have an excuse for not answering me young lady?"

"Oh, did you call?" she asked with innocence and heard a snicker in the background.

"If your name is Adelle I did!"

"My name is Carmen." She said sweetly smiling up at the astonished face above her.

"Carmen!" Mrs. Sutton sputtered as she reached out and grabbed her by the ear and lifting her from her desk commanded.

"Go to the principal's office at once and explain to him who you are, Missy."

Closing her book and placing it below her desk she marched from the room, head held high, such as a regal queen named Carmen might do. Mrs. Sutton watched, then turned from the class hiding a small smile and sighing whispered, "What is to become of that girl?"

Adelle dawdled as she made her way down the hall her resolve crumbling. This was the second time in a month she sad been to Mr. Harvey's office. She didn't want her father to hear of it and he and Mr. Harvey were friends. She needed to think this through, what was she going to tell Mr. Harvey?

Drawing on a resourceful imagination and thinking of conversations she had overheard between her mom and Aunt Addie she pushed open the door and sadly shook her head as the principal looked up. Biting at her lip she tried working up a tear or two.

Noting her distress Mr. Harvey stood and rushed forward putting out a consoling hand.

"Hear-hear what is the problem Adelle. Are you alright?" he asked in a kindly voice placing his arm gently around the tearful girl.

"It's Mrs. Sutton." She whispered, "I think she is going through the change and has gone completely mad."

Pulling back Mr. Harvey studied her face thoughtfully then asked, "What makes you think this Adelle?"

"She called me Carmen when she knows my name is Adelle and then sent me here for no reason." Sneaking a look at him she went on, "You know women just are not themselves sometimes during this stressful time in their lives. Some even have to be institutionalized." She finished with a nod of her head.

Leaning against his desk he put his hand to his face as though considering all she had said and to cover the laugh he was holding in.

"I suppose I will have to look into this situation. Maybe I should go have a talk with Mrs. Sutton."

"Well there is no telling what she might say. You need to be real careful around women who are in that state of changing."

"I will remember to follow your advice Adelle; you stay here while I go speak to her."

Feeling confident he believed her story Adelle looked around the office with interest. Moving from her chair she tried out Mr. Harvey's seat. Discovering it spun around she took a few turns and noticed a door in the corner she had never seen before. Wondering where it might lead she took a quick peak. Stepping inside she found she was in a storage room where the big boiler sat that provided heat for the school. Investigating where the many pipes led she suddenly realized Mr. Harvey had returned along with Mrs. Sutton. Not anxious to face them she remained very quiet.

"Now where did she get off to?" She heard the principal ask.

"I don't know Paul, but something needs to be done about that girl and the tall tales she comes up with." She laughed, "Last week her name was Gwendolyn, this week it is Carmen. Each week it is something different."

"She's just going through a stage. I'll speak to her Dad about it when we play golf tomorrow."

Hearing this Adelle was so upset she failed to hear Mrs. Sutton when she said, "She is very intelligent and creative far beyond her years. I think she is bored with the class and needs to be moved up a grade."

"Could be, her Dad owns a small newspaper and I think he has had her helping him since she was a toddler. I'm sure that would account for a lot of it." He remarked as they left the room.

She couldn't figure out what went wrong, she was certain Mr. Harvey had believed her. She studied on it and decided it must be those big boobs Mrs. Sutton had and maybe she had a tail too.

She had heard her Dad say all men liked big boobs and a little tail. He had been talking about their new neighbor, Dolly. She had been very observant since that time but had seen no evidence she had a tail.

She knew SHE didn't have one. Maybe that was it; she was a freak, different from everyone else.

She thought of her hiding place under the front porch. She loved to lay there and listen to all the grown-ups talk about things her mother said little ears should not hear. Some of it was hard to understand but now and then it was interesting.

The bell rang and she could hear the students rushing through the hall laughing and talking as they changed classes. She would just lay low a bit longer until she was sure 'the Mister' had not come back to the office.

Finding an old chair that had been removed from the teachers lounge and awaiting its trip to the dump, Adelle sat down and started planning what she would tell her dad about being sent to the office. Did men go through that changing thing?

She woke with a start. It was late she could tell by the light coming through the small window past the furnace. How long had she been in there? She ventured into the office room and peered down the hall.

Feeling a tinge of panic when she realized she was alone in there she quickly shook it off and wandered into the vast hall. It was kinda spooky, there was not a sound but her own footsteps and they echoed in the quiet building. She had the urge to prowl around but seeing it was so late she knew she better get home. Going to the door she found it locked. How was she to get out? She went to the exit door at the end of the long hall they used when they had a fire drill. It was locked too. A window would have to do she decided, but soon found they were locked from the top and she had no way of reaching the latch.

Now she began to feel uneasy. She was going to really be in trouble if she couldn't get out of the building. Her Dad would skin her alive! No excuse would be good enough. She had to get out. She though of the little window in the storage room, maybe it would open. Running down the empty hall to the storage room she imagined someone was behind her and she quickly closed the door once inside, her heart was pounding. She listened but heard not a sound. Dragging a straight backed chair to the door she wedged it under the knob so no-one could follow her in, then hurried to the window. It was too high for her to crawl through. She didn't even know if it would open. She looked around for something to stand on. A box that was to small, decorations, stage props, and band instruments, nothing suitable to stand on but the chair she had used to hold the door shut. She would have to use it. She approached the door with caution. What might be on the other side? She felt a thrill of fear as she reached for the chair. Grabbing it she quickly drug it to the window and climbed up, she still could not reach it! Maybe the little box would help. She glanced toward the door, was the door knob turning? Shivering with fear she jumped down and snatched up the box, placing it on the chair she scrambled to the top and giving it a shove the little window came open. She struggled to get through the opening. She couldn't do it. She stopped and tried to think what she could do. She thought of her Daddy. What would he say? Never say never is what he would say! Where there is a will there is a way! She thought a minute then took off her shoes and threw them through the window, getting a firm grip on the metal window casement she walked up the wall with her stocking feet and pulled herself to the opening, wiggling through.

    Exhausted from the effort she lay on the ground. It was almost dark. She had to hurry! Slipping her feet into her shoes and looking around to see just where she was she took off running toward third street. There seemed to be a lot of traffic and people walking around. A lot more than usual. Were they looking for her? If they were she knew she was in deep dodo.

    In an attempt to avoid being seen she decide to cut through the cane field on the corner of third and Marsh just two blocks from her house.

    It looked scary. The street lights had come on and dark shadows were cast across the path that was usually bathed in sunshine when she went through. Taking a deep breath she ran like the devil himself was reaching to grab her. Though she felt a sharp pain in her side and she was breathless she didn't stop until she reached the back porch of her home. Very carefully she opened the screen door praying it wouldn't make the screeching sound it usually made, for once it opened quietly, with relief she shut it gently and stepped into the kitchen. She could smell something good to eat but decided if she could make it to her bedroom with out being seen she would climb into bed and pretend she had been there all along. As she stepped into the hall her mother called out, "Adelle is that you? I left your supper on the back of the stove." Her mother stepped into the hall and flipped on the light. "Goodness how did you get so dirty."

Her mother's gentle hand stroked her face as she smiled sadly," I Guess they haven't found the little Morris baby yet?"

All Adelle could do was look into her mothers trusting face and half way nod while wondering and hoping she would tell her more about what was going on. The Morris baby belonged to that Dolly woman with the big boobs.

"I hope they find him soon. I would hate for him to stay out in the damp night air for very long. Some are afraid he has been kidnapped."

Kidnapped! The fear she experienced running through the cane field came to Adelle. They had been warned over and over to stay out of there, that homeless people and winos lived among the dense patch of cane and some of them might not be nice.

"Eat your supper and get ready for bed."

"Tomorrow is Saturday." Adelle reminded her in protest. When her words seem to fall on deaf ears,

"Where is Daddy?" she asked nonchalantly.

"Out with the men looking for the baby."

Adelle pictured the chubby three year old alone and scared, maybe in the cane patch. She shivered.

She picked at her food still worried about her Dad and the principal meeting. Pushing her plate back but picking up a fresh-made cookie she went to get ready for bed. Her mother came in to say goodnight.

Adelle snuggled into her cover relieved she had bypassed her Dad so far.

"I think it is good what you did today." Her mother said as she sat on the edge of her bed and tucked the blanket around her.

Surprised, Adelle's sleepy eyes popped open wide. "Excuse Me?" she thought.

Her mother seeing her puzzled expression explained. "Spending your afternoon with your school friends looking for the baby."

Is that what happened? They turned school out early so we could all look for little Leroy? Gee I wish I had been there instead of locked in that old schoolhouse. She silently swore, I will never tell about that!

"Goodnight, sweet dreams, say your prayers and remember the lost baby."

Feeling a little frightened and certain she would never fall asleep; she stared at the sheer curtain as it fluttered at the window, was there something out there? Her eyelids felt heavy, she blinked trying to stay awake. Try as she might she couldn't stop the sleep from sucking her under.

Soon troubling dreams began of dark places and the cane patch, of being scared and running and falling over something, it was baby Leroy. She cried out but no one could hear her. No one would listen. She was in a panic, she needed help but it seemed no-one could see her. She pulled at their clothing and begged. Opening her mouth to scream no sound came out!

She woke with a start; her usual happy mood on waking was missing, replaced with one of dread. She heard voices in the kitchen, from that she figured out Leroy had not been found and they were losing hope he would be found alive. She remembered her dream but not all of it. It was disturbing and she worried and felt cross. Dressing she went to the kitchen, several neighbors were there at the kitchen table with her Dad. They looked tired. Mama was pouring coffee. They all stopped talking when she came in the room.

"Adelle you need to look after your brothers this morning while I go sit with Mrs. Morris for a bit, poor woman." Adelle saw tears in her mother's eyes; it made her hurt deep in her chest to see her mother so upset otherwise she would have put up a fuss about watching the boys. This was Saturday for gosh sakes! She had plans to climb and explore on West Mountain.

Little brothers were such a pain, especially Robert! Billy was just a baby so he wasn't so bad. She loved him but she wasn't sure what she felt about Robert he was a pest and always into something.

She had begged them to take him back to the hospital after they brought him home. All he did was cry and demand attention. If it had been Robert that disappeared instead of baby Leroy, probably no body would have looked so hard to find him. They would have said good riddance!

Seemed Mama was partial to Robert. She couldn't figure that out? She was four years old when the stork left him at the hospital with a nametag on his toe and instructions to call her Mama and Daddy to pick him up. Once you picked up a baby they wouldn't let you return them Daddy said. Sounded like a bad deal to Adelle. They probably wanted to get rid of him too, but now THEY were stuck with him!

Mama had them fed and dressed and ready to go play. Adelle took them out on the porch and put the baby in his playpen. Robert sat on the top step playing with his toy car.

"Don't get the notion you can get off this porch." She cautioned as she watched him ease down a step, that said she turned her attention to baby Billy. Next thing she knew Robert was down on the sidewalk. "I told you to stay on the porch. I'm gonna tell Mama you won't mind. I hope she whips your scrawny little butt, Robert." She said glancing over her shoulder wondering if anyone had heard her. Mama didn't like her talking like that but he made her so mad. Picking Billy up she put him in the carriage and eased him down the steps where she could keep an eye on his big brother. By then Robert had moved to the curbing around Mamas flowerbeds running his car in the soft dirt.

"Don't mess with Mamas flowers." She warned and proceeded to push the carriage down the sidewalk to the corner and back.

"Oh no!" she wailed, Robert had pulled some of the flowers. "Your really gonna catch it now, mister." she said smugly relishing the thought.

Settling down on the step where she could keep an eye on him she patted her foot impatiently thinking of where she would be if it weren't for these two little brats. Time seemed to drag by. Then she noticed two women walking in her direction from Main Street. When they drew near she asked, "Is there any news of the Morris Baby?"

Surprised by her mature manner they stopped.

"No, nothing yet."

"What a cute little boy." one of the women cooed at Billy.

"Yes, he's mine." Adelle replied possessively.

"Oh, and who is this handsome little man over here?" The other lady asked with a smile. Robert gazed at her with his big blue eyes and grinned his cute little boy smile. Adelle hastened to answer,

"Him, he doesn't belong to us. He was left on our doorstep and is adopted." Cutting her eyes at Robert she wondered if she could give him away.

The women exchanged glances.

"And what is your name?" one asked.

"Beatress Faye." She replied without hesitation. "I am much older than I look."

"I see, and isn't this the Dennis residence?"

"Yes, I am visiting. I live in Long Island. That is a long way from here."

One of the women laughed.

"Tell Mrs. Dennis hello for us. Beatress Faye, that's a lovely name." the lady said in a kind voice as she studied Adelle's face. The look made Adelle feel uneasy and for just a moment she regretted what she had said. She watched them as they walked away wondering who they were. Did they know her mama?

Adelle jumped as her mother stepped out on the porch, the screen door slamming behind her.

"Adelle I'm back." She said as she sat down on the porch steps and held her arms out to Robert who ran to her with his fist full of her prize flowers.

"I picked these for you Mommy." He said proudly handing them to her.

"Well thank you Robert, they are beautiful." She said hugging him close. "How sweet you are to your Mommy." Her eyes were full of tears.

"Yuk!" Adelle exclaimed in disgust and disappointment as she turned away.

"I'll take the boys with me now honey. You can go play with your friends."

She didn't want to play with her friends; she was going up on the mountain. She might sneak through the Calvary camp on top and go to the lake on the other side and dig for crawdads along the waters edge.

She could visit with the old couple who lived at the fishing camp. She liked to hear the stories they told. Someday she was going to travel all over the world too, just like they had. The old woman had been an actress she said. Adelle thought she would like to be an actress also and sing and dance on the stage.

Her mind made up she started up the slopping street to the foot of the mountain, past the rock boulders and scrubby oak to the fence that surrounded the Calvary unit. Ignoring the NO TRESPASSING sign she crawled beneath the fence and ran across the road just missing a troop as they cantered past. Running through the trees, hiding now and then she pretended she was being chased by a gang of outlaws, she scurried beneath the next fence enclosure and breathlessly came out on the path that led to the lake shore.

Running down the path and along the waters edge she made her way to the cabin where her lake friends lived. She instinctively knew Alma was not the type of woman her mama would approve of her being friends with but there was an air of excitement about the bold red haired woman. She had been so many places and seen so much and Adelle loved to listen to her tell of her adventures.

Passing by their old green pickup truck loaded down with boxes and bedding it never crossed her mind that they might be leaving until she knocked on the screen door and saw the suitcases sitting on the porch.

Alma called out, "Come on in I'm in the kitchen. This should be the last of the food stuff." Turning she was noticeably surprised when she saw Adelle standing there.

"Well now aren't you a surprise." She said and looked past her. Adelle turned to find Ernest standing behind her.

"Are you going someplace?" Adelle asked.

"Yes, Ernest got a new job and we will be leaving today." Alma acted funny and kept looking at Ernest.

Adelle felt really sad about losing her friend. "I wish you wouldn't leave."

Ernest spoke up, "Yeah, we hate to go but we gotta get a move on . . . Alma!" He jerked his head toward the other room and glared at Alma.

They sure are acting weird she thought.

"Well honey I don't have time to visit, I will miss you but I have a lot of work to do to get ready to go, so you better run along. When we come back I will drop in to see you." Adelle didn't believe her. Alma stood and walked to her and placing her arm around her shoulders proceeded to guide her toward the door. As they passed through the small front room Adelle caught sight of a small figure moving in the corner. At first she didn't know what it was, but when her eyes adjusted to the darkness she saw it was a little boy lying on a palette asleep. She stopped and looked at him.

"That's my nephew Sammy. We're taking him to his mama in Chicago."

Adelle walked closer and studied him. She knew right off it was Leroy. She could feel Alma and Ernest watching her. Prickles of fear clutched at her. She felt the hair crawling on her neck. She swallowed hard.

"He sure is a cute little boy." She said and turned toward the door. Ernest reached out and put his heavy hand on her shoulder. She froze and looked up into his frowning face. He looked toward Alma and then removed his hand.

Adelle turned and threw her arms around Alma and began to cry. She knew Alma thought it was because she was leaving but it was really because she was scared out of her wits. Alma gave her a hug and Adelle turned and ran from the house. Her heart was hammering in her chest. "They were stealing Leroy! She had to get some help!"

She had to hurry; they were almost ready to leave. She slipped and slid as she climbed to the summit and the fence enclosure. She had to sneak through; she couldn't afford to get caught now there was no time.

How was she going to explain how she knew this? She had been forbidden to go over the mountain to the lake or through the military academy.

She couldn't worry about that now; she just had to get some help. Scooting across the top she slid down the mountain at top speed not even slowing when the thorn bush grabbed at her dress and tore her skin, she had to save Leroy.

Robert's big blue eyes flashed before her. They could have taken her little brother; she felt her blood surge and knew she would never have allowed that to happen even if he was a pest.

Once she cleared the rocks and brush she went sailing down the street past the church and before she reached the house she was screaming for help.

She crashed through the door "Mama, Mama! I found Leroy!" Her mother came from the kitchen, her father and several men behind him. One was her principal. Oh no! She thought briefly. Out of breath she gasped again, "I found Leroy, some people at the lake have him and they are packed up and leaving right now! We have to hurry and stop them!"

They all just looked at her.

"We have to hurry." She said again as she looked into their doubting faces.

"How do you know this Adelle?" her father asked.

"It doesn't matter how I know I just do and you have to hurry or they will be gone." She cried, tears running down her face mixing in with the dirt and sweat from her ordeal.

"Adelle are you telling the truth this time?" Mr. Harvey asked.

"I swear it's the truth."

"Who are these people?"

In a rush of words she told them, "Alma and Ernest. They have an old green pickup and it is packed and Leroy is asleep on a palette on the floor and they were ready to leave when I got there."

"You were at the lake?" her mother asked in surprise.

"Please Mama you have to believe me." her mother studied her face. "I believe you Adelle."

She fell into her mothers arms and then jerked back and whirling around looked at her Daddy's face. She could see he was trying to decide. She pleaded with her eyes. He reached out and hugged her. "Alright sissy . . . ." Then turning to the others as he picked up his hat he said,

"Let's go get Leroy."

Adelle anxiously waited for the men to return. Would they get there in time to find Leroy? They sat on the porch and waited, Mama holding Billy and Robert leaning against his big sister, her arm placed protectively around his stocky body.

They saw the police car as it turned the corner, trailed by many others, and headed their way. Jumping up they followed it next door as Leroy was delivered to his sobbing mother. Adelle felt a lump in her throat and couldn't say a word when they hugged and thanked her. She figured she was in big trouble anyhow as she had disobeyed her father but she couldn't help but feel happy.

The following Monday they had a special assembly at school and Adelle was asked to come to the stage. The Mayor and Mrs. Morris and Leroy were all there. Her mother and Daddy with Robert and Billy were there too. Mr. Harvey called her to the center of the stage and there in front of the whole school and a lot of the town people he awarded her with a medal of honor for saving Leroy. Then he asked "Now what is your name?"

Seemed everyone held their breath before she sheepishly replied . . .

"Adelle Dennis and I am nine years old." she added as she looked out in the audience at the woman she had fibbed to about her age, "and I will never tell another whopper!" she said as she crossed her fingers and smiled.

© Bodrury 2009

"Writers Block"

"Dad-nab-it!" came a frustrated cry, sheets of paper flew across the room and fluttered to the floor near an untidy pile scattered around a wire trash-basket. An aged figure of a man slumped dejectedly into a desk chair as he ran his fingers through his wiry white hair. Stubble of whiskers covered his troubled face as he gazed out the window into the gloom of an overcast day.

Oblivious to the antics of the young kid goats playing in the pasture, he brooded over his failure to come up with a story he was to write. He glanced toward the calendar near his desk and noted once more the big circle drawn around October 5, the deadline for his story.

Sighing he rose from his seat and with a noticeable limp walked to the open fireplace across the room and reaching out to the heat warmed his stiff fingers. It was time to take a break. Taking his pipe from the mantel he packed it with aromic contents from the Prince Albert tin and using a small twig from the edge of the fire lit it; puffing until he was satisfied it was going well.

As he scanned the bookcases before him, among the many volumes was an old one, frayed and dog-eared from many readings, by Mark Twain. Reaching for it and settling into an easy chair near the warmth of the fire, he opened to the first page. A smile came to his face as he read about Aunt Polly, for he too had an Aunt Polly. He chuckled at the description of the young hooligan in her charge and how he used and tricked his friends into doing his work, and then there was Jim, he had known him, too. How parallel his life had run with this tale written so many years ago.

He dozed as he read; drifting into a dream of days long past, days of happiness, when he was a lad of ten on his uncle's farm, back in the hills of Oklahoma.

"Why are you doing that for?" questioned a timid voice.

He turned and looked into huge blue eyes filled with tears.

"Why am I doing what for?" he asked, unsure of what he had done to distress the little blonde girl watching him.

"You just killed that worm." She answered accusingly.

"Well how else do you think I can go fishing if I don't hook the worm?" He replied in disgust. Avoiding her tearful face he lightly tossed the hook out over the water.

Watching thoughtfully she inquired, "Will it hurt the fish when he bites the hook?"

Uncomfortable now, he shrugged his shoulders, "Naw, fish don't have feelings."

"How do you know that?"

Angrily he turned to her, "Who are you? Go away, you're scaring the fish." Turning his back to her he watched the red float as it bobbed gently on top of the water.

Girls, they ruin everything. He could feel her watching him. He secretly hoped the fish didn't take his bait while she was there. He turned once again, fully intending to say something mean to her, but when he saw the tears running down her cheeks he was suddenly tongue-tied. Pulling in his line he packed up his fishing gear and as he got up to leave she followed. They walked along in silence. He gave her a sidelong look.

"What's your name?" he asked, wondering where she came from.

"Amy."

She was younger than him and small. He suddenly felt very protective. Reaching out his hand he said, "Come on, I'll walk you home." Her hand was little and soft, he looked at her face, she smiled, it gave him a funny feeling in his stomach. He smiled back.

Awakening and opening his eyes they focused on a small portrait across the room of a laughing young girl in a white dress. A signature at the bottom read,

Love forever, Amy.

With a smile lingering on his face, he sat the old book and cold pipe aside and rising he walked to his desk with a spring in his step. Settling down in the well worn chair and glancing again at the photograph he began to type with renewed vigor. He had his story, thanks to Amy and Mark Twain.

© Bodrury 2008

"My Dad, My Hero"

The year was 1936. Farrington community, ten miles from town, had a one room school house. This particular year there was only one little girl old enough to attend first grade. Her name was Jeannie. She was to become my best friend. She was eight yrs old. I was five. Not quite old enough to go, but the school board approached my parents and asked them to allow me to start early. Though I was young, I was eager, and so I began my education that fall.

Our teacher, Mrs. Lewellyn was a lovely woman with dark hair, a sweet voice, and a sunny disposition. All the children loved her. Each row of desks was a different grade, one through six. There was no one in the second grade but a couple of lively boys were in the third. It was all very exciting learning to do numbers, the alphabet, and writing. But the very best was the art table and the songs we learned and making new friends.

One cold winter morning heavy dark clouds began to roll in from the north and covered the bright blue skies. The wind began to howl around the school building and the bitter cold moved in. We were busy with our lessons and paid little attention, but Mrs. Lewellyn was aware of it and watched closely as conditions worsened.

When lunch time arrived she gathered up our lunch boxes and doled out half of what we had. By then ice and snow had begun to fall. We had our turn at running out to the outdoor privy and hurried back inside. The bigger boys helped her bring in wood for the fat bellied stove that sat in the center of the room near her desk.

We watched as the snow began to build up on the window sills. To the children it looked like a winter wonderland. To our teacher it looked like trouble.

As the day progressed the snow deepened. Our teacher let us play games of I spy with her diamond ring and we gathered around the piano and sang songs. We thought it was worlds of fun but as evening came and the snow had piled around the building and the wind continued to howl and we could not see anything for the heavy snow it was frightening. I wanted to go home.

Mrs. Lewellyn got out our lunch boxes again and got down her tin of cookies that she saved for special occasions and made it seem like we were having a party. She had a teakettle on the stove and made us all tea and though it seemed a festive affair the desire to go home was uppermost in my mind.

Soon the lamps had to be lit and the cold from the big windows seeped into the room. We gathered around the stove to keep warm and she held me on her lap as she read stories to us. My heart ached and my stomach hurt and I wanted my Mama but I would not cry. I was not a sissy. I fell asleep and Mrs. Lewellyn wrapped me in my coat and placed me on the art table with my friend Jeannie.

We woke to a bright, white, still world. The snow had stopped. As far as we could see there was nothing but snow. Mrs. L. made us more tea and passed out some of her treasured cookies. Then one of the bigger boys looking out the window said he saw something moving down the road. We all rushed to see. It was just a black dot moving slowly toward us. As we watched we could see it was a tractor, soon we could see a man behind the wheel. He was all bundled up in a big coat and had a cap that covered his ears and a scarf over his face. He pulled up in front of the school building and tramped through the crusted snow to the front door. It wouldn't open. A snow drift had it blocked.

The big boys inside pushed and the man outside pulled; it began to move a little. He scooped the frozen snow away but some fell inside as the door opened. Cold air swooped into the warm room. The man stepped inside slapping his cold hands together. Ice had formed on the scarf across his face from the moisture of his breath. He took off his gloves as his eyes swept the room, Reaching up he pulled the scarf from his face. "Daddy" . . . His arms opened wide and I leapt into them releasing the tears that I had held all night.

Soon other tractors came down the road and between my Daddy and the other fathers all the children were taken home. We were the last to leave the school that day. Mrs. Lewellyn locked up the door after she made sure the fire was banked and safe. She bundled up and Daddy took her down the road to her home with me riding on his lap. He had come after me and led the way through the drifts of snow and Ice. I was his little girl. He was my Hero. Always was, always will be.

© 2007 Bo Drury

"The Odd Box"

Ann had just moved into the new house. Boxes were everywhere. Chaos reined. Would she ever be straightened out? After living in the country for thirty years and with all the things accumulated, she didn't think so. She had gotten rid of many things she thought she'd never part with, but the boys thought it best she move to town. The big house was a lot to take care of and they thought she spent too much time alone. So what she couldn't give away she sold and here she was in town and alone! What had changed?

The kids were proud of the house they helped pick out and it was nice but Ann wondered if it would ever feel like home? She already missed the old place. No looking back she told herself. She had been telling herself that for three years, ever since Sam had left her so unexpectedly. It was lonely, especially at night. She tried not to think of it. She had all this unpacking to do; it would keep her busy for a while.

She looked around, it was late, too late to start now. Noticing a box she didn't recognize she started to check it out but decided she was tired and it could wait, all she wanted now was a shower and to crawl into bed. Tomorrow would be a better day.

After a restless night in strange surroundings she was up early and on the patio with coffee when two of her granddaughters came in to help. Deciding what was to be done, she asked first, for one of them to see what was in the odd box. Digging it out they discovered it was full of photo albums. "Gran-ma who are these people?" After looking them over, Ann didn't know them either. Turning to Becky, she said "Look at these and see if you recognize any of them."

"Where in the world did you get these Gran-ma, these are the Parker kids. I went to school with them. They lived east of town. How did you end up with this box?" No one knew. It was decided a phone call would be made first to the moving company, in case the Parkers were looking for the box, and then the Parker family.

The rest of the day was spent trying to make some order in the house. The girls wore out early and each one had other things to do and places to go, so amid hugs and kisses they promised to come back another time.

Ann sat down and propped her feet up. They had made progress. Pictures were hung, beds were made, and dishes were in the cabinets. As she gazed around the room her eyes rested on the strange box. I may as well call now she thought. They are probably frantic over their pictures.

Finding the phone book she looked up the Parker's number. There were three of them with a 538 prefix. The first was no longer in service. She got up and made tea and came back to dial the second number. On the third ring a man answered.

"Mr. Parker?"

"Yes."

"My name is Ann Dickson. I have just moved into town and somehow I ended up with a box that belongs to your family. A box of photo albums. I was afraid you might be worried about them so I wanted to call."

There was silence on the other end of the line.

"Well Miz . . . what did you say your name is?"

"Dickson."

"They must belong to my grandchildren. I'll let them know. How do they contact you? Where are you located?"

"It's a new address," she explained,"915 Red Oak. They can call me at 723-1350. I'm most always home."

Another silence, then,

"I would come myself but I just lost my wife recently and don't get out much."

"Oh, I am so sorry Mr. Parker, I do know how you feel, I lost my husband some time ago."

Another silence, then,

"I know a lot of women do not like to tell this, but how old are you?"

Surprised Ann laughed." No, that's okay, I am seventy three."

"Well, I am older than you but I'm in real good shape." He laughed, "Maybe we could have dinner together sometime?"

Completely taken back Ann didn't know how to respond.

"Maybe . . . sometime . . . we'll see."

"I'll tell the boys about the pictures."

"Okay Mr. Parker. Goodbye."

Ann hung up laughing, the very idea, the old flirt. Just wait till I tell the kids the old guy 'made a move on me'. With a little giggle she headed for the kitchen thinking of the conversation. She walked with a new bounce in her step. She felt like a silly schoolgirl.

The phone rang.

"Hello."

"Miz Dickson, this is Tom Parker, I was just thinking, maybe I could come and pick up the box myself, no telling when the boys would get around to it. If it would be okay with you, that is?"

"Of course Mr. Parker."

"When can I come?"

"Maybe Sunday after church?"

"That would be good and Miz Dickson . . . . has anyone ever told you what a beautiful sweet voice you have?"

© 2007 Bo Drury

"The Move"

"Those BASTARDS"

Those words shouted by my angry father jerked me awake instantly, my heart pounding, as I knew something was dreadfully wrong. I saw him pass my room with his rifle in hand and my mother close behind.

"Abe be careful" Grandmother was putting on her robe and my brother was close behind her. I jumped out of bed wondering at the noise I could hear from outside, the continuous roar of large motors. Running out the door and onto the porch I peeked around my grandmother who was cautioning my father to be careful, I saw a pasture of heavy equipment in the way of bulldozers and tractors lined up to the north of the house and barn.

Daddy walked out into the yard and raised his rife and pulled the trigger sending a shot into the air. It got the attention of the man in the nearest tractor. He raised his arms and began to climb down. Another man jumped down and in his hand I saw a big wrench. Dad leveled the 30 30 at him and the first man motioned the second fella back, then held up some papers and came forward, his hands still in the air.

Dad shouted, "First man who moves one of those tractors forward gets a belly full of lead. Now get that stuff off my property."

The man with the papers approached him and handed him the sheaf of paper. Dad motioned for Mom to come forward and handed them to her while he kept his eyes on the men in front of him. Mama read the papers to him. Dad's body language was enough to tell us he was really upset. We could see him arguing with the guy and Mama trying to calm him down. The man turned and headed back to the tractor and motioned for the men to cut the motors. There was a sudden quiet. Dad put his hand to his face and Mama put her arm around him. They turned and came back to the house. I looked at my grandmother, her lips were set in a firm line and her black eyes were snapping.

Dad looked like a man defeated. He was quiet for a few minutes studying on what to do next. No-one said anything waiting for him to speak.

"I have to get the others together and go see the judge. We have to get an injunction against them and give us time to move off the farm." He looked around at the home and land they had shared for these past eleven years, it was all he had, the land he inherited when his dad died, then he looked back at Mom. He reached out and ruffed up Buddy's hair and looked at me. I could see the hurt in his eyes. "They condemned the farm. They can do that, bulldoze our barn, tear down our house, take our inheritance, the damn government can do anything they damn please and there is nothing we can do about it, especially now during wartime."

He went inside to put away his rifle and get his hat, then came out and got in his truck. We all stood there watching, first Daddy, then the men who were getting into government cars that had driven up, they left driving out across the wheat field they had destroyed earlier with their trucks and tractors.

I went into the house and found Mama wiping tears away from her face, Granma patted her on the shoulder and went to our bed room to dress, Mama turned to me and held out her arms. I didn't know what to say, I was scared. What was to become of us? Where were we going? I had lived in this house for eleven years, all my life.

Buddy came in and marched into his room and came back with his bb-gun and slingshot, a determined look on his young face.

"Don't be going and getting your self into trouble young man." Mama warned.

"They better not push me around." he muttered as he went out the door. We watched him as he went out the door and headed for the barn.

"How in the world are we going to move all this?" Mom asked of no one in particular looking out across the yard at the chickens and other animals grazing in the pasture. "Does anyone want something to eat?" Everyone is always hungry during a time of crisis.

"How about a little coffee." Granma said as she came back into the kitchen tying on her apron. "Then we still have chores to do." She stated matter-of-factly. "Albert will take care of it."

It seemed forever before Daddy came back with a writ that gave us time to move everything from the farm. First he had to find a place. He had a plan. Just like Granma said, Daddy was gonna take care of it.

The story above is true, maybe not accurate in word for word but the events took place as I have described them as I remember it. It was a very emotional time and disturbing. The land was used to build an airfield and base for the military. Perhaps my brother can add what he remembers to the story. I hope he will. I am sure there are many things I have forgotten or left out but this is a bit of family history.

Our neighbor harvested his crop riding with a shotgun across his lap until he was finished. They didn't move their house but he saved his wheat.

* * *

A family that had a place right on the edge of the confiscated property and unused pasture land for miles into the canyon below them let Daddy lease the land and he started making plans to move down there. There were several old barns, a three room bunkhouse, and a windmill with good water. It was really kinda exciting after we got over the first shock of it all. He took us along and let us think we had a say in picking out the most perfect spot for the house. A dry creek ran along the west side and there was a small pond with a big willow tree beside it and down south of the house there was a bunch of cottonwood trees. It was totally different from the flat land around our farm house.

First he had to find some movers to jack up the house and prepare it to be moved. We packed everything and got it ready to go. Daddy had put up a pipe fence around the house and it had to come down so the moving trucks could get in close.

He sat the house on high ground in the canyon and planted the trees he dug from the old place around it. The house was placed on cinder blocks off the ground and faced the south so in the summer it could catch the cool breeze that swept through the canyon. The back side of the house had only one window and it was in their bedroom facing north.

Next they moved the big barn and set it behind the one that was already there. Some of the buildings were so old they could not be moved.

It was a pretty place and when you first drove over the hill and caught sight of the white house with the green roof and trees around it nestled in the canyon it was impressive. We loved it down there and called it the 'Valley Ranch.' I still think of it as home even now after all these years of being away. Mother and Daddy loved it and reminisced often about the time we spent there.

Although we were only eight miles from the little town of Lefors we went to school in Pampa which was a twenty mile drive from our house. We rode the first ten miles by private car driven by our 'school-bus' driver Mrs. Gladys Davis, a neighbor who lived in the old Davis school house at the head of the canyon. Most of the Davis farm land had gone to the government also. The last ten miles into Pampa was by a regular school bus. During the winter we left for school while it was dark and got home after dark.

Besides having the sheep and cattle ranch Daddy opened a meat market in town and made sausage. Naturally it was called "Valley Ranch Sausage". It was fun for us as we got to hang around town in the afternoons after school.

The 'Rex' theater was just down the block and Saturdays it was the cowboy show matinee. We just had to go each weekend, the cost was .09 cents. No way were we gonna miss the latest episode of the continuing serial. Right down the street on the corner was a drugstore that always had chocolate cake; I loved to get a slice with a dip of vanilla ice cream. Besides a fine array of pirates and cowboy pistols that my brother and I loved to look at and dream of owning they also had what they called a lending library where you could rent books to read. That's when I got hooked on mysteries . . . Nancy Drew and Ellery Queen.

Then Dad got into the building business and started building houses. The war was over and the service men and women were coming home and the boom was on. He bought three lots and built three houses on Nelson Street. After selling the first two he decided we would move to town so we moved into the third house.

Here we are packing up to move again. Daddy gave up the lease on the ranch and jacked up the house and moved it to town also, Of course we left everything else but personal items and the tools and tack and took with us wonderful memories of living on the Valley Ranch.

Daddy set the old farm house on a lot near the high school and added on to it making it a beautiful two story home which he sold to one of the Reynolds family. Ironically that family had bought the big Tallyhone ranch from Grandmother years before after Gran-dad died. It is now owned by Boone Pickens, a wealthy rancher-oil tycoon.

When we are young we think things are forever. Now we know that is not so. Everything goes in time but the memories we hold so dear. That is really all we own that belongs just to us and we can keep for a lifetime. Share them and hold them near to your heart . . .

"Adrift"

Susan rolled over with some effort and looked out across the lake. The sun was high. "It must be noon." she thought, idly watching the light play patterns on the motion of the water. She had the window open wide and propped up with a stick trying to catch what breeze she could. It was too hot to move. The water looked cool and inviting. She toyed with the idea of swimming but was afraid she would sink like a rock. She looked down to her belly huge with child. "Just one more month." She sighed.

She couldn't wait to be slender again. Maybe it would be like it was in the beginning for her and Jody, right now it was awful. He stayed gone all the time. She thought she must look so ugly he couldn't stand to look at her. She never thought it would be like this. Tears welled up in her eyes. She didn't know where he went each day. He hardly spoke to her at all any more. She just hoped he would be there when her time came. Her folks thought they were married and so did his mama. She was a sweet woman. Susan knew she didn't like the way Jody treated her, but she couldn't do nothing about it. She came out to check on her when she could. It was a long way and her car was old. She had taken her to the doctor when she found out about the baby. They gave her a little book too read and told her she was healthy. They gave her a list of vitamins to take and told her to come back in a month, but they never had any money, so she'd never gone back. Jody didn't see any reason for her to go as long as she felt ok.

Her back hurt so bad, Jody said that's 'cause she laid in bed too much, but there wasn't nothing else to do. She was uncomfortable sittin' up so she had to lie down. There wasn't nobody to talk to either but the old couple down the road. Jody said if she needed help she could walk down there and the old man would take her to town.

She wished her Mama would come out and get her and take her home but Daddy wouldn't let her. He was still mad 'cause she ran off with Jody. She told them they got married. She had begged Jody to go along with her story. She knew her Daddy would have whupped her good for going out and spending the night with a boy. She had felt the broad side of his hand before and couldn't stand the thought of his anger. If Mama stood up for her she would catch it same as she would. Jody had said he loved her so it was logical to her that they live together.

He hadn't counted on her getting pregnant at all, but then neither had she. He hadn't said much when she told him. He acted kinda proud at first, but then she had been so sick. Every morning it started and lasted all day. He stayed away more and more. When she got sick while he was around, he'd put his coat on, get in his truck and turn the stereo up real loud.

The old lake shack they lived in had been cold all winter. At first it didn't matter how cold it was, they'd just pile on some more cover and snuggle beneath it laughing and giggling and playing around. Jody would jump up out of bed in the mornings and run to the wood burning stove in his bikini underwear, throw on a log and jump back in bed with his cold feet on her. They had stuffed all the cracks with rags to keep out the wind and when it rained the rags soaked up the water and ran down the walls. Now the rags were water stained and brown. It hadn't been built for winter living but it was all they could afford. Jody just made a hundred dollars a week at the gas station. He paid out most of that on his pickup. That pickup meant more to him than anything in the world. It had a roll bar and spotlights and he kept it polished to a high shine. Susan felt a little jealous of that truck. She knew it meant more to him than she did.

The baby kicked and squirmed inside her. She watched as a little knot raised the tight skin across her stomach and slowly moved to the other side. She stroked it gently. She'd heard it could hear her voice and she talked to it a lot. Sometimes she sang just to hear another voice. The baby and the old radio was all the company she had most days.

She crawled to the edge of the bed and lowered her swollen feet to the floor. Little prickles of pain traveled from her feet to her ankles when she touched them to the cracked linoleum floor. She'd had to go barefoot since her shoes cut into the swollen flesh on her feet. She reached for Jody's shirt tossed across the iron railings at the foot of the bed. When her clothes began to get too tight for her, she had to wear the big shirts. For a while she could wear her jeans unbuttoned, but now she had nothing but these to wear. It was lucky it was summer. She shuffled to the cook top and lifted the bent lid off the steaming pot of beans. They smelled good but she sure would like something else. Seemed like they lived on beans and potatoes. Jody did bring her a coke now and then. She used to think she had to have one for breakfast every morning.

She wondered what her friends were doing. She had missed going to school. She never thought she would say that, but it was true. She wished she could see her friend Tina. Tina thought what she had done was exciting. She'd like to tell her like it really is, awful!

She had just started her sophomore year in school when she met Jody at the skating rink. He was so good-looking and paid attention to her right away. Dad wouldn't let her wear makeup 'til she was sixteen, but that was more than a year away. Tina carried a bag of makeup everywhere she went and would fix her face for her. With her face done she looked much older than fourteen. She'd filled out by the time she was thirteen and her Dad preached to her all the time about getting into trouble. You'd think having a nice body was a curse listening to him. Jody was out of school and had a job and had plenty of money all the time and that dreamy pickup. He didn't mind spending money on her either. It was enough to turn a girls head. She didn't tell Jody how old she was for a long time. He cussed some when she told him, but by then it really didn't matter. He had seemed some surprised when he found out she'd never been with anyone else.

Susan walked to the door and pushed open the screen to stand on the porch. The door banged shut behind her, sounding extra loud in the quiet summer day. All the sounds seemed magnified that day. The screeching of the bedsprings when she moved, the sound of the clock ticking, the sizzle of the beans boiling over on the stove and the big green flies buzzing in and out the screens on the windows. She had laughed when Jody tried to put tape on all the holes poked in the screens to keep out the flies and mosquitoes. It looked like Band-Aids sticking on 'em, but the first rain washed 'em off. After that he just let them come and go when they wanted too. Sometimes they had to pull the sheets over their heads at night when the mosquito's were extra bad. He brought home some 'Off' and it worked pretty good but the smell of it made her sick and she was scared it might hurt the baby somehow.

She walked to the lake trying to step on grass and weeds to keep the hot sand from burning her feet 'til she got to the waters edge, then stood ankle deep letting it soothe and caress the taunt skin on her feet. She brushed away the hot sand on the shoreline and carefully lowered her heavy body to sit in the cool of the damp sand. She squinted against the bright light on the water, closed her eyes and leaned back, feeling the warmth of the sun on her skin. The waves lapped against the shore and washed over her feet and legs in a rocking motion. She felt drowsy and relaxed; she drifted in and out of a light sleep. Somewhere she could hear a dog barking and the sound of a hammer striking metal, making a ringing sound like a buoy-bell. She dreamed of being in a boat far out in the water, all alone, with no paddle, set to drift about forever. She woke with a start thinking of the beans on the stove. She rolled over and clumsily got to her feet and hurried up the path to the shack. She had to stop halfway up to catch her breath. She had stayed in the sun too long and had blistered. Her back ached and she had a pulling sensation nagging in her stomach, it felt good to get out of the sun.

The beans were almost dry; it's good she woke up when she did. She wanted to shower and look nice when Jody came home tonight, she felt lonely. She had read those same old love story magazines over and over again.

She put her hand to her stomach, it was hard. The baby was balled up in a knot. It made her back really hurt. Maybe the shower would make her feel better. She knew Jody was tired of her feeling bad all the time. The warm water burned her skin where it was blistered, but it felt good to wash away the sand and sweat and feel the smoothness of her skin. The baby kept knotting up in a little ball making her uncomfortable. She brushed back her hair and put the blue ribbon in it that brought out the blue of her eyes. She used some of the baby powder that Jody's Mother had brought out for the baby. She put on a clean shirt. She wanted Jody to like the way she looked. She tried not to think of all the pretty girls he saw every day. The ache in her back had turned into a drawing sensation that lasted a few seconds each time it came. Was it a pain she wondered? It was too early. The baby wasn't due until July. Jody said he was going to call it "Firecracker". She wished Jody would come home. She felt suddenly frightened remembering the dream she'd had down by the water. How alone she felt. She wished she could talk to her Mama. She felt like crying. The pain came again. She looked down the road hoping she would see the shiny black pickup. There was nothing. It was a half-mile to the old couple's house. The pain started again. She started to cry. She would have to walk barefoot in the hot sand of the road. She hated Jody! It was his fault she was pregnant. She cried harder. She stood in the middle of the room looking around, tears streaming down her face, her hands to her stomach wondering what to do. She saw an old pair of tennis shoes Jody wore when he went fishing sticking out from under the bed. She leaned over to pick them up. The pain started again, she leaned against the bed. She shivered and her teeth chattered. She clenched them tight, trying to keep her chin from quivering. The tennis shoes were stiff from being wet. There was sand caked inside as well as out. Susan hated putting her feet in them, but she couldn't stand to walk in the hot sand and there would be grass burrs on the side of the road. She was still shaking although it was a hundred degrees outside and not much cooler inside. Her jaws and neck ached from clamping her teeth together. She looked around wondering if she should take anything with her. She didn't have anything. As she went out the door she thought of leaving Jody a note, but where was he? He should be here she thought. He doesn't care what happens to me. The thoughts brought on a fresh torrent of tears making it difficult to see the path before her. She had to stop when another pain came, then walked on, crimping her toes to keep the large tennis shoes on as she trudged down the sandy road to the neighbors' house.

    The old man saw her coming from where he sat on the front porch.

"Mama," he said to the old woman kneeling on the ground working her flower beds. She looked up to see him nod his head toward the lake road.

"Here comes that girl. Looks like she might be in trouble."

The wiry little woman got to her feet and turned to the figure coming toward them. Taking off her cotton gloves she shaded her eyes from the afternoon sun and watched the young woman hesitate, her hand to her back.

"Better get out the car, Pa, looks like we may be going to town." She brushed off her clothes and walked to the gate to meet the girl. One look at the tear stained face and she held out her arms and enfolded Susan in a comforting embrace.

"It'll be ok. Pa has gone for the car. We'll take you to the hospital and call your folks. Wait right here." She said leading her to a bench under a low branched mesquite tree. She returned shortly with a cool wet wash cloth and her old leather purse. She handed Susan the cloth to wipe away the grime mixed with the tears smudged on her face.

The old man had backed the car to the gate and had gotten out to stand by the door. He avoided looking in Susan's direction after noting how skimpily dressed she was. The shirt she wore barely met over the stomach pushing out in front of her and her pink bikini panties rode so low he wasn't sure she had on anything at all. It was hard for him to keep from looking." Poor little kid, sorry husband she has." he muttered. They were well aware of how much time she spent down there in that old shack alone. They couldn't help but notice since the road ran right by their house. They weren't nosey neighbors, but there wasn't much to do out like this and though they were not conscious of it, they had a habit of watching the young couple. In some ways looking out for the young girl. They didn't think much of the young man the day he stopped by in his fancy black pickup and shiny boots. He asked them to keep an eye out for her since her time was coming near. His hair was slicked back and smelled of hairspray. His beard was trimmed real neat and he had wax on his mustache. The old man said he never did trust any man that hid his face behind a beard, and a mustache made him think of a villain in the ole time movies. Only man he ever liked with a mustache was Clark Gable.

He sneaked a look at the girl. She looked so young and her big stomach made her look so small, that and those big old shoes. His opinion was that the boy should be horse-whipped!

The old woman walked with her to the car. The old man opened the door to the backseat and waited, eyes averted, while she climbed inside and leaned her head against the seat. Closing the door he reached to open the door for his wife.

"I can do it, Pa. Let's go." She said hastily watching the girls face as another pain began. The old man hurried to the drivers' seat, put the car in low gear, and carefully let out on the clutch, worrying about the rough ride ahead of them on the bumpy road.

"Hurry, Pa, times getting' short." The old lady said, reaching back and taking hold of Susan's hand, squeezing gently in reassurance.

Nothing else was said during the fifteen mile ride to the hospital. The pains continued but they didn't last long.

The old man pulled into the emergency room entrance and the woman helped Susan from the car. An orderly seeing them arrive, rushed out with a wheel chair. The old man drove away to park. Susan clung to the old woman's hand as the orderly pushed her inside and stopped at the registration desk. A young woman looked up, smiled briefly, and asked Susan if she could answer some questions or if she needed to go on in. Susan nodded. The girl behind the desk looked to the old woman, wondering if the nod meant "yes, she felt like answering "or "yes she needed to go on inside." Understanding the look the old woman bent to Susan and asked quietly.

"Girl, can you answer her questions?"

"Yes." She nodded.

"Give me your name please." the young clerk said in a professional tone," starting with the last, then first and middle initial." She spoke with fingers poised above the typewriter keys.

Susan hesitated. What should she say? She wasn't married to Jody, would she be in trouble if she lied? She could feel the tears coming. She wished her mother was there, she'd know what to do.

The young typist looked up, impatience showing on her face. She saw the tears in the girl's eyes. She looked to the older woman who was watching Susan. She saw the old man come to stand beside them. She asked the couple, "What's her name?"

The old woman looked uncomfortable. Leaning toward the girl again she asked,

"Girl, what's your name? They need your name."

She whispered, "Susan Marie."

"Last name first, Pleeze!" the clerk said visibly irritated.

Susan's eyes were big, fear showing in them as she watched the woman behind the desk. She'd been taught not to lie, even though she had at times to her parents, but this was different. She pictured a courtroom and this woman as the judge and her sworn to tell the truth, the whole truth, and nothing but . . .

"Roberts," the name burst out loud in the quiet of the hospital corridor, "Susan Marie Roberts."

"Age?"

"I'm fifteen." The words came out soft but clear. The typist looked up to study Susan's face.

The old man turned away exclaiming, "I'll be damned! She's just a baby herself." As he went to sit in the corridor waiting room. The old woman shook her head.

"Father's name, puleeze. Last name first." She added hastily.

Susan lowered her eyes wishing she didn't have to answer that question. Why couldn't the baby just be hers? She knew the woman was waiting.

She looked up meeting the woman's gaze," His name is Wright, Jody."

The woman looked away and typed. She kept her head down. She met all kinds here in admitting. It was best to type and feel nothing, but it was hard to do sometime. She felt sorry for this little girl. Where were her folks and where was her boyfriend? She asked,

"Your address?"

"The old Lake Road." she answered.

"Its route two," the old woman spoke up.

The clerk typed quickly, "Zip code?"

"76301" the old woman answered.

"Your next of kin?"

Susan thought about it for a minute, "My parents, George and Faye Roberts. I want to call them," she stated. The clerk looked up, opened her mouth to speak, but the old woman spoke first.

"Tell me their phone number Susan, I'll call them right now." Susan gave her the number, then said

"Ask my Daddy to please let Mama come. I need her bad." Her bottom lip quivered and her words were shaky. She frowned as another pain came. This one was harder and lasted longer. She shut her eyes and waited.

The woman behind the desk sat quietly watching Susan's face and decided to let her go on to labor and delivery. She nodded to the young orderly. He started to push her down the hall.

"Wait," the clerk called out, "Who is your doctor?"

Susan stared at her blankly. She had no doctor.

"I can't remember his name," thinking of that one visit.

"You have to have a doctor," the woman protested.

"I don't," Susan said simply.

The woman raised her hands in exasperation. The orderly waited.

"Take her on, I'll do something," the clerk said watching Susan as another pain started.

The old woman hurried from the pay phone to catch up and follow down the hall.

"Your folks are coming Susan. Everything will be just fine now." She said reassuringly. When they reached the elevators, she leaned over and kissed Susan on the cheek and brushed back a strand of hair that had fallen away from the blue ribbon. "Pa and I will stay until your folks get here. We won't leave you." Susan's frightened eyes held hers as the orderly pushed her into the elevator and the doors closed between them.

The old woman sighed and walked back to her husband.

"There's a waiting room on second floor maternity," the woman behind the desk volunteered to the old couple, then watched as they made their way to the elevator.

She dialed maternity to let them know they had a patient on the way with no doctor. "Let them worry about it," She said aloud.

The next few hours were like a nightmare to Susan as she drifted in a half-sleep. Partly from exhaustion, partly from medication to dull the sharpness of the pain. There were always faces looking down on her, probing, pushing, asking questions. Once she saw her mama's face with her Daddy behind her. He looked sad and tears were running down his cheeks. He called her name and said he loved her. She knew that was a dream. She felt her mother's cool hand on her face. It felt good to see her Mama. She bathed her face and put chips of ice in her dry mouth.

The bed was hard and she wanted to turn over but that big old stomach was in the way. She told them she wanted to go home; she was tired of all this, but no one would listen to her. Those women in white uniforms whispered at the foot of her bed. They upset her Mother. God, her back hurt. She didn't think she could stand it any longer. She didn't want to act like a baby but she needed to scream and holler so someone would help her. She screamed. A nurse threw back the sheet and hurried from the room. She came back with a man. Susan wanted to cover herself but the pain was too bad. Her body was consumed with it. She gritted her teeth and tried to push away from the pain. She couldn't get away from it. A nurse rushed in." Don't push," she said. An orderly came in with a stretcher. They began to lift her too it.

"No," she screamed," I can't move my legs." She looked about frightened. The man was Dr. Pace. She clutched at his arm. He would help her. He had always helped her when she was a little girl.

"Do something." she begged.

"It'll be over soon Susan," he said gently, as they rolled her down the hall. She saw her Mother watching, her hands together like she was praying. She thought she saw her Daddy, but she knew it wasn't him. He hated hospitals and besides he was mad at her.

They moved her to a different bed. It was even harder. They strapped her legs apart. Her back hurt. She needed to turn over. She tried to fight, to get up. She tried to reach, to grab that terrible pain. She couldn't stand it. They grabbed her arms and strapped them down. She had to get up. Why were they being so mean to her? It had to be a dream she thought. Someone put something over her face. She choked and tried to push it away. She turned her head away from the sickening smell. It followed her. A voice said, "breathe deep, Susan, breathe deep." She gasped for breath, tired of fighting. She began to drift away. They took the mask away, "No, No!" she thought, "Put it back." She wanted to slip into the black nothingness of sleep. A voice called to her.

"Help us Susan. You have to push now . . . now Susan . . . Push! That's right; you're doing good, Susan." She had no control over the bearing down, the pushing. She wanted to scream but she was not in control. Bright lights exploded around her. Flashes of yellow and red. She heard someone scream, again and again. She wondered who it was. Everything was lights and faces moving about, around, and above her. It was a dream she was sure and soon she would wake up. The mask came back. She breathed deeply of the sickening sweet smell, welcoming the feeling of drifting into the gray whirlpool pulling her down, down, down. She was in a boat far out in the water, spinning round and round, about to go under—she would drown. NO! NO! She screamed. She heard someone call.

"Susan—Susan, its over. You have a little girl."

"Are they crazy?" she thought, "I am a little girl. I want my daddy." She cried as she sank into the black nothingness.

Susan roused from a deep sleep to roll over on her side. Something was holding her arm. She was tangled up. She opened her eyes to see a plastic bag hanging by her bed, a tube leading to her arm taped in place.

Had there been an accident? She wondered, did I nearly drown? No, I had a baby she remembered. A baby, it wasn't a dream.

She looked over to see her Mother across the room, her head bowed, unaware Susan had opened her eyes. Susan quietly watched her, and then let her eyes travel the room to rest on the figure of a man silhouetted against the window. It was almost daylight. The sky was pink and blue behind him. The man stood very still his hands behind his back, seemingly lost in thought. He looked familiar to her but it was dark in the room. He turned, the dim light from the hall caught his face.

"Daddy." She whispered.

He started, surprised at her speaking, then came forward to look down on her. He looked tired and haggard. A soft smile came to his face, but he looked sad. He took her hand in his and stood searching her face.

She felt frightened. Was he still mad at her, or worse, because of the baby? She watched him, afraid to speak. Why was he so angry with her all the time? It didn't used to be that way. She had always been Daddy's little girl until a couple of years ago and then he changed. He didn't like her growing up. She couldn't help that. She wished it could be like it was before he stopped loving her. He didn't say anything, just looked at her. She began to fidget under his gaze.

Her Mother rose and walked to the bed reaching out to smooth back Susan's hair. She smiled a smile that told her everything was okay. She glanced back to her father.

"When you are able, you're Mother and I want you to come home with us," he spoke huskily. "We'll work things out. It will be okay."

He turned and left the room hurriedly. Susan knew he was crying and couldn't understand why.

"Susan," her Mother said, watching her closely," how do you feel?" She nodded, not knowing what to say. Finally she asked, "Is Daddy still mad at me?"

"No your father loves you very much, Susan." She hesitated." There is something special between a father and his little girl. He was afraid of losing you."

Susan suddenly remembered the baby, "I have a little girl. Where is she?"

"Susan, she was so tiny."

She felt a sudden fear.

"Was . . . ?"

"Honey, I am so sorry." Grief showed on her face, not for the tiny little figure that had struggled to live through the night, but for this child of hers, half woman, half little girl, that had suffered so to bring her baby into the world only to lose her, never having the chance to cuddle and love her, never to know her.

Susan stared dry-eyed at her Mother. The baby she had cradled inside her, had talked too and sang too . . . she turned away and looked through the window as a new day dawned. Looked out across the city towards the lake where she had lived and carried the baby for eight months and now . . . nothing! "This is part of that dream," she thought, closing her mind to the truth, "I'll wake up soon."

She tried desperately to sink into oblivion. The dream came to her again, of drifting alone, aimlessly upon the water. So all alone. She began to cry . . . to sob . . . grieving for her baby, her lost innocence, and Jody, her first love.

© Bodrury 2008

The following is for the very young or young at heart!

"BOOKS"

There's love, adventure, and knowledge
for all of us to share.
But treat these books with kindness, and
handle them with care.
There's many a thought and effort
written in each page you read
It sets your mind to working and
gives your thoughts a lead

To many an adventure on
land and on high seas,

To the very deepest forest
And through the greenest leas,

You meet the meanest pirates,
Dressed in black and with their gold;

And all the brave frontiersman
who fought in days of old,
Who cleared the path and paved the way
so their stories can be told.

You learn of dogs so brave and true,
A friend to man and child.
And of their fiercest enemy a-living
in the wild.

88

88

You read of horses big and strong,
Prancing with heads held high,
Racing like the wind itself
Silhouetted against the sky.

Travel through the canyons deep,
With shades of purple and blue
Then climb the mighty mountains,
And take a friend with you.

A whole new world has opened up
To travel as you please.
Just turn the page and lose yourself
It's done with so much ease.
You can lounge around in an easy chair
Or sit beneath the trees

With crickets singing their chirping song
And feeling a touch of a breeze.

But no matter what you're reading
You travel at your pace.
You may wet an eye, or cheer a heart
Or have a smile on your face.

Now when you've read your story
And learned the things you lack,

Then close the book up carefully
And gently put it back.

For another soul may come along and
Have a mighty need
To fill his life with adventure
And find a book to read. © BODRURY 2008

Get Published, Inc!
Thorofare, NJ 08086
23 February, 2010
BA2010054